"Are you going to make the supreme sacrifice for your sister?"

Cassie blinked. "Sacrifice? What are you talking about?"

"Aren't you about to offer yourself in your sister's place?" Justin drawled smoothly. His dark eyes were back on her face now, pinning her startled gaze.

"To be honest, Mr. Drake, the thought never crossed my mind." Her voice was clipped and angry. Take her sister's place as his bride? What a ridiculous idea. "I doubt that you'd find me a satisfactory substitute, anyway!"

"If by that you mean you're not sufficiently sweet and biddable and capable of learning to do as you're told, don't worry about it. I'm sure that with a little practice we could come to a suitable arrangement. I'm a reasonably patient man and I'd be willing to work with you until you got the role of wife right."

STEPHANIE JAMES

is a pseudonym for bestselling, award-winning author **Jayne Ann Krentz**. Under various pseudonyms—including Jayne Castle and Amanda Quick—Ms. Krentz has over twenty-two million copies of her books in print. Her fans admire her versatility as she switches between historical, contemporary and futuristic romances. She attributes a "lifelong addiction to romantic daydreaming" as the chief influence on her writing. With her husband, Frank, she currently resides in the Pacific Northwest.

JAYNE ANN KRENTZ

WRITING AS
STEPHANIE JAMES

NIGHTWALKER

Silhouette Books

Published by Silhouette Books
America's Publisher of Contemporary Romance

SILHOUETTE BOOKS

ISBN 0-373-80695-7

NIGHTWALKER

Visit Silhouette at www.eHarlequin.com

Printed in U.S.A.

One

The danger in dealing with Dracula was that even as she tried to ward him off, a woman found herself wondering what it would be like to have him make love to her.

Cassie Bond stood at the edge of the well-dressed crowd and surreptitiously eyed the dark-haired, dark-eyed, darkly dressed man who was dancing with her lovely blond sister.

Dracula. Everything about Justin Drake reinforced her image of the man as a creature of the night. His hair, black as a moonless evening, had just enough silver at the temples to hint broadly at his age. Drake had recently turned forty. Heavily lashed and sensuously narrowed, his unfathomable eyes were dark, bottomless wells. When he looked at her sister Alison, Cassie told herself sardonically that it was impossible to tell whether he wanted to kiss her or sink a pair of fangs into Alison's slender throat.

Strong bones defined Drake's arrogant, harshly carved features. There was no hint of softness in the hawklike nose or the grimly etched mouth. That mouth bothered Cassie more than a little. She had never seen Justin Drake laugh or even smile sufficiently to display his teeth the way normal people did. Probably because he didn't want others to see the traces of blood, she decided. Drake did occasionally smile but his mouth always seemed to twist in a manner that was as disquieting as it was primitively sensual. And when the smile appeared it was never spontaneous, but rather coolly calculated, deliberate.

Justin Drake did not appear to make unnecessary movements, but when he did move there was a feline fluidity about him that made everyone around him appear a bit uncoordinated. It was unnatural, Cassie told herself irritably. It was unnatural for a man who was forty to have a body that was so hard and lean and graceful. It was unnatural for a man to wear elegant black-and-white evening clothes with so much assurance and authority. It was unnatural for gentle, lighthearted Alison to be so fascinated with a man who exuded lethal sensuality and menace the way Justin Drake did.

All he lacked was a black cape, Cassie decided. Put Justin Drake in a cape and you'd have a dead ringer for Count Dracula. She winced at her unwitting use of the word *dead.* Then she took a long sip of her white wine and frowned fiercely. Her imagination was going into overtime.

But, damn it, how could Alison act as if she were half-hypnotized by the man? Didn't she see the danger in him? Or was that part of the attraction? Regardless of her younger sister's apparent fascination, Cassie knew she was going to have to put a stop to Drake's seductive courtship. The man was a fortune hunter; an experienced, ruthless male who would take advantage of Alison's naïveté to take control of her money. A modern-day Dracula if ever there was one.

Cassie Bond knew all about elegant, interesting fortune hunters. Her fingers tightened violently around her glass. She would not let Alison become a victim. Her twenty-three-year-old sister belonged with the man she had been in love with since she was sixteen: Mark Seaton. If Justin Drake hadn't appeared on the scene two months ago, Alison and Mark would now be making wedding plans.

Cassie drew a long breath and forced herself to relax. Tonight she would act. Matters had gone on long enough. There was no point in hoping that Alison would grow bored. In fact, things were rapidly approaching the dangerous stage. Cassie had begun to live in fear of hearing the announcement of her sister's engagement. No, tonight was the night. Cassie had at last found a way to ward off Dracula and she intended to use it. There was danger involved but Alison's future was at stake. The risk would have to be undertaken and the sooner matters were resolved, the better for all concerned.

There was no one else around to shoulder the responsibility of protecting Alison. Cassie's aunt and uncle were out of town on an extended world cruise. Her parents were dead.

She made her way along the fringes of the crowded hotel ballroom, which had been rented for her sister's twenty-third birthday. The laughing crowd was, in large part, composed of people who were younger than Cassie. The couples around her tended to be in their midtwenties, although a few approached Cassie's age of thirty. Barely. And almost none of the guests were as old as Justin Drake. For good reason— all of the people were Alison's friends. Cassie wondered why her sister didn't question Drake's lack of personal ties. He never introduced her to anyone in his own social sphere.

Cassie's lips curved in contempt. She knew very well why Drake didn't bother introducing his prospective bride to his friends. Justin Drake's acquaintances couldn't stand the light of day any better than he himself could.

As she moved through the crowd of well-dressed San Franciscans, Cassie knew that, unlike Justin Drake, she was a part of this elite group. Her dress was a soft fall of tiny pleats done in ruffled white chiffon and belted with a small cord at the waist. It had a designer label inside and it was accompanied by the most delicate of white sandals, straight from Italy. The gold at her throat and on her wrist was very real. The cost of the total outfit had been exorbitant, but that was all right. Cassie could afford it.

Unfortunately, the overall effect of luxury and polished glamour was, as usual with Cassie, not echoed by the basic woman underneath the sophisticated clothes. As Alison had often affectionately remarked, if ever a woman had been born for jeans and a T-shirt, that woman was Cassie Bond.

Even tonight, after an arduous afternoon at an expensive hairstylist, Cassie's carefully styled hair was coming loose from its moorings. The shoulder-length golden-brown mass had been beautifully cut, shaped and anchored in a sleek curve to the back of her head. Now, one hour into the evening, long, wispy tendrils were already trailing down the length of her neck. The precisely positioned coil of hair had somehow gone slightly askew and no longer had the perfectly shaped configuration Gerard had worked so long to achieve. He would be stricken if he could see the results of his labor. But there was nothing Cassie could do about it. Her hair had a built-in mechanism designed to demolish any style forced upon it.

The subtle, blended tones of copper and wine that had been applied by Gerard's makeup artist and guaranteed to last twenty-four hours were already looking a bit smudged. With philosophical resignation Cassie accepted the fact that the elegant makeup would not last the promised length of time. She'd be lucky if most of it hadn't somehow worn off by the end of the evening. Makeup always seemed to wear off quickly on her. The mechanism that made it smudge and quickly disappear was no doubt allied to the antistyle forces in her hair.

But while it lasted, the subtle makeup highlighted a brilliant pair of amber eyes. Wide, delicately slanted, brimming with intelligence and an appreciation of being alive, Cassie's eyes were the focal point of her face.

It was a lively face, full of animation and interest that made people forget the absence of beauty. The mouth smiled easily, even when it was painted in bronze and gold as it had been that afternoon. The colors on her lips were disappearing as rapidly as the rest of her makeup, so the mouth underneath would soon be back to its natural rosy color.

Cassie had the slender, supple body needed to wear the rippling, pleated dress; but somehow the gown didn't look quite right on her. Designer dresses that cost as much as this one did ought to be worn with an air of cool sophistication and a hint of arrogance. Cassie gave the impression of wanting to rush home and change into her jeans. It wasn't that Cassie personally liked the supercasual look. As it happened, she didn't care for it at all. But it clung to her with amazingly perverse tenacity.

But she wasn't thinking of her appearance as she made her way through the crowd. Cassie Bond was intent on cornering the dark, dangerous man who had been courting her sister with single-minded intent. The confrontation could be put off no longer.

As the music came to an end another man approached the striking couple on the dance floor and requested the next dance with Alison. Justin Drake relinquished her with an intimidating air that implied that many such interruptions would not be tolerated. He seemed to realize, however, that he could hardly refuse to let others dance with the woman in whose honor the party was being held, and he moved off the floor with his unusual fluid stride.

Cassie watched anxiously. She didn't want to lose track of him now. He was headed for a quiet, glass-walled alcove designed to provide a seating area away from the music and activity in the main ballroom. Picking up the long skirt of her gown in one hand and still clutching her wineglass in the other, Cassie hurried after him.

The alcove was lit with only a discreet lamp designed to resemble candlelight. After the glittering brilliance of the ballroom area, it took Cassie's eyes a moment to adjust to the shadows. The first thing she saw as she came through the doorway was the outline of Justin Drake's dark figure silhouetted against the array of city lights outside the window. A creature of the night, she found herself thinking once again.

"Mr. Drake?" Something about the frightening stillness of him made her more uneasy than ever. He stood with his back to her, apparently contemplating the cityscape. Cassie had met him on two previous occasions but then only briefly. Now he answered her inquiry with cynical graciousness, not bothering to turn around.

"Call me Justin, Cassie," he drawled far too gently. "It seems appropriate under the circumstances, don't you think?"

"What circumstances, Mr. Drake?" Summoning up enough determination to overcome the strange reluctance she was experiencing, Cassie moved a couple of steps into the room. They were alone, she realized with a tingle of trepidation, and then she immediately chastized herself. She wanted to do this in private, didn't she? Blackmail was much better conducted in private.

"You're going to play the protective older sister, aren't you, Cassie?" He continued to gaze out the window as if the scene below were far more interesting than her presence. It probably was, Cassie admitted to herself. But that would soon change.

"What makes you think that, Mr. Drake?"

She couldn't see his face but she had the impression Justin was smiling one of his twisted, dangerous smiles. "Ah, Cassie. Did you think I wouldn't notice the way you glared at me when we were introduced last week? Or that I didn't see the glint of fury in your eyes this evening when you arrived?"

He turned away from the window at last and Cassie's suspicions about his smile were confirmed. In the shadows his dark eyes seemed compelling and totally unreadable. "My intentions toward your little sister are completely honorable, you know."

"That," she said distinctly, "is exactly what I'm afraid of."

He regarded her in silence for a moment. The man had a way of infusing even his silences with poised menace. "You're an odd little creature. Do you know that?" He glided forward a pace and examined her as she frowned up at him. "If I didn't know better I'd say you'd been grappling with some man in a secluded corner of the hotel. You look rather pleasantly mussed."

"You don't know me at all, so you're hardly in a

position to speculate on how I pass my time at parties!'' she snapped, infuriated. He had no business looking so elegantly at ease in his expensive clothes while she was beginning to fray around the edges.

He shook his head once in an amused, negative gesture. ''I've only met you twice, but I'm fairly good at sizing up people. And I think it's a good bet you aren't the type to let yourself get into a brawl with some overeager admirer. One glance from those golden eyes and any man who had stepped out of line would probably melt. You have an interesting way of conveying a lot of contempt in a single look, did you know that?''

''You don't seem to be melting,'' she observed dryly.

''Meaning you've been giving me that kind of look all evening?'' he murmured. ''I know. But you see, I'm not like most of the men you know.''

''I'm well aware of that. Which is precisely the reason I wanted to talk to you in private.''

''About your sister.''

''About my sister,'' she agreed firmly. The small alcove was positively alive with uncoiling threat. Cassie could feel the tendrils of it as they reached out to curve around her. Confronting Justin Drake was every bit as bad as she had thought it might be. Too bad she hadn't worn a necklace of garlic. Wasn't garlic supposed to ward off vampires? Or was that for werewolves? She was a little hazy on the matter. ''I'll come right to the point, Mr. Drake. I want you to leave Alison alone.''

''I see.'' He appeared to give this some thought,

his dark eyes searching her intent face. "That's blunt enough, I guess. You have some definite reason for wanting me to back off?"

"She's in love with another man; a man she's known since she was sixteen. If you hadn't appeared on the scene and swept her off her feet two months ago, she would have been engaged to Mark by now."

"Really?" Justin Drake smiled a little blandly. "There didn't appear to be any other man in the picture when I arrived."

"Only because she and Mark had argued. They've argued on and off for years. It means nothing. But this time you were there during the period when she was determined to show poor Mark that he didn't own her. And somehow…" Cassie's voice trailed off as she realized she didn't know how to explain Alison's continuing interest in Justin Drake. Her sister ought to have been running back to Mark weeks ago. Justin seemed to have hypnotized her.

"I want her, Cassie." The statement was flat and final. Cassie shivered, a part of her wondering what it would be like to have a man make such a statement about her instead of Alison. She could only be glad the implicit demand was aimed at someone else, even if it was Alison. If it had been aimed at herself, Cassie knew, she'd already be fleeing the small room.

"You're not going to get her, Mr. Drake." She tried to make her own voice equally flat and equally final.

He stared at her a moment longer and then he turned back to the window. "You're going to make

an interesting sister-in-law, Cassie." It was a direct
challenge and they both knew it.

"I'm not going to let you marry her."

"I intend to do exactly that. Your sister has something I want very badly, you see."

"I'm aware of that. You're not the first man to eye
her money."

There was a pause. "She is also a very beautiful
woman," Justin finally pointed out.

"I'm aware of that, too. You're not the first man
to have noticed her looks, either. A nice combination,
hmm? Beauty and money."

"And youth. Aren't you going to remark on that
aspect of the situation? I can't believe you'd let it go
by unmentioned."

"I'm glad you realize you're too old for her," Cassie shot back grimly.

"I intend to marry her, Cassie," he whispered.

"Are you pretending to be in love with her?" she
challenged. Cassie was getting more and more nervous by the second. She'd never taken on anyone
quite like Justin Drake and she knew she was flying
blind. At any moment he might turn away from the
window and attack. An image of Justin sinking
gleaming-white teeth into her throat flashed through
her mind. Desperately she tried to banish the picture.
"Surely you aren't going to be that hypocritical?"

"Why not?"

"Are you saying you're in love with her?" she
pressed.

"Does it matter? Would you stop trying to scare

me off if you thought I was deeply in love with your sister?'' he asked curiously.

"I would never believe you're in love with her!''

"Then there's no point in discussing that particular issue, is there?''

Cassie drew a deep breath and grabbed for both her patience and her fortitude. "Mr. Drake, I would just as soon stop fencing with you. I'm asking you to leave my sister alone. Since your main interest in her is money, I'm willing to approach the subject from that angle. How much?''

He blinked. It was like watching a large night animal lazily blink at potential prey. *Not me, Justin Drake,* Cassie thought. *You're not going to hypnotize me.*

"Bribery, Cassie? Isn't that a bit, er, tacky?''

"Don't play games with me. How much do you want to leave my sister alone?''

"You couldn't possibly give me enough to compensate for the total I'll lose by not marrying your sister, can you?''

"It was worth a try,'' she told him, lifting her chin aggressively. A few more tendrils of hair worked loose from the sophisticated coiffure.

"Perhaps.'' He smiled humorlessly. "But I'm afraid I'll have to let the offer pass.''

"It's your last chance, Mr. Drake. If you don't take me up on the offer tonight, I won't make it again.'' She knew he would refuse. He was absolutely right, of course. She couldn't afford to compensate him for the total amount he'd lose by relinquishing Alison. But there had always been the chance he might seize the opportunity of making a lot of money fast and avoiding marriage at the same time. "Think it over, Mr. Drake. If you take the bribe, you'll still have a tidy sum and you'll avoid the ties of matrimony. Somehow I don't see you as a married man," she added dryly.

"You don't think I'll make a good husband?" One black brow rose.

"Frankly, no. Do you?"

"I'm prepared to perform my duties."

"I'll bet. Look, Mr. Drake, I'd appreciate it if you would just give me a yes or no answer."

"I already have. The answer is no." He seemed to be waiting, as if he were genuinely curious about what she would do next.

Cassie hesitated, trying to discern some sign of uncertainty or anger or any other readable emotion in his hard face. But Justin Drake simply watched her. And waited patiently for whatever she intended to do next. It infuriated Cassie. She found herself longing to attack him physically, to know the primitive pleasure of wrapping her fingers around his throat and squeezing until she got some kind of human reaction.

"You don't leave me a great deal of choice," she finally said quietly. Her amber eyes held his dark gaze resolutely.

For a moment longer he continued to study her and then Drake let his eyes glide downward; along the length of her throat, over the curve of her small breasts, past the flare of her hips and all the way down to her toes. Cassie realized vaguely that she was glad the pleated skirt fell to her ankles because the stocking on her right leg had a run in it. She didn't like the idea of confronting Dracula while trying to conceal a run in her panty hose. The image lacked dignity.

"Don't tell me, Cassie, that you are going to make the supreme sacrifice for your sister."

It was Cassie's turn to blink. "Sacrifice? What are you talking about?"

"Aren't you about to offer yourself in your sister's place?" he drawled smoothly. His dark eyes were back on her face now, pinning her startled gaze.

"To be honest, Mr. Drake, the thought never once crossed my mind!" Her voice was clipped and angry. Take Alison's place as his bride? What a ridiculous idea. "I doubt that you'd find me a satisfactory substitute, anyway!"

"If by that you mean you don't think you'd be sufficiently sweet and biddable and capable of learning to do as you're told, don't worry about it. I'm sure that with a little practice we could come to a suitable arrangement. I'm a reasonably patient man and I'd be willing to work with you until you got the role of wife right."

Cassie's mouth fell open in outraged astonishment. Then she realized what was happening. "You're trying to bait me, Mr. Drake, but you're wasting your time. Go ahead and enjoy what humor you can get out of the situation, but I'm warning you, in a few minutes you won't find anything very funny!"

Black lashes lowered over his dark eyes, concealing what little of his gaze she had been struggling to analyze. "I'm crushed, Cassie. Don't you think I'd make you a satisfactory husband?"

"About as satisfactory as Dracula! You're after money instead of blood but you'd do just as much damage in the process!"

His lashes lifted and that faint, tormenting smile etched his mouth. "What a lurid imagination you have. What sort of man would you prefer as a husband?"

"There isn't any sort of man I would prefer," she gritted, wondering desperately how they had gotten off onto such an idiotic topic. "I tried marriage once, Mr. Drake, to a man who had a few things in common with you, as a matter of fact. I will not make that mistake again!"

"You'll never marry a man like me again?" he queried, as if trying to clarify her response.

"I will never marry again! Full stop! Do you understand, Mr. Drake? Can you get that through your head?"

"Once burned, twice shy?"

"Completely shy! And fortune hunters are at the top of my blacklist. Now, if you don't mind, I'd like to continue with our original discussion. I don't want to waste the whole evening standing in an alcove arguing with you."

He went to the window again, lifting one hand to brace himself easily against the wall as he gazed out at the city. "You're not having any success bribing me and you're not going to offer yourself in your sister's place. So what is there left to discuss, Cassie?"

She wished he sounded a little upset or angry. But Justin Drake's voice was as dark and deep as the sea, giving away nothing of its secrets. She drew a long breath. "How about the little matter of your past?"

The stillness in him became more absolute for an instant and then he turned slowly to face her. Cassie shivered as the level of danger in the small room rose by a factor of at least ten. If it hadn't been for Alison, she knew she would be flinging herself out of the alcove and back to the safety of the crowded ballroom. Her palms were damp, her breathing was shallow and her head was throbbing with the beginnings of what could easily turn into a major tension headache. Maybe she was having an anxiety attack, she thought bleakly. Anybody facing Dracula was certainly entitled to one.

"If I recall the legend correctly, Count Dracula had a rather extensive past," he finally noted calmly. "Are we going to go into great detail?"

Cassie kept hold of her temper. "Your immediate past will do, I think. You see, I know all about the casino you owned until last year, Mr. Drake. I know about your odd assortment of friends and business acquaintances and I know that the further I look into your past the murkier it gets. As far as I'm concerned you're little better than a gangster and if you persist in trying to marry my sister, I'll see to it that she and everyone else in her circle of friends is made aware of that fact!"

Having dropped her one and only bombshell, Cassie unconsciously chewed on her lip and waited for the result. Blackmail was a new field for her and she wasn't quite sure how to continue now that she'd issued her ultimatum.

Drake regarded her obliquely for a long while, as if assessing and analyzing her. Then he finally said, "You seem to have done some research."

"I did. I hired a private detective. It wasn't hard to find out you'd owned a casino in Nevada. Once we knew that..." She let the sentence trail off meaningfully.

"Once you knew that, you jumped to all sorts of conclusions, didn't you, Cassie?"

"I didn't exactly jump to the conclusions. Most of them were fairly self-evident facts. Such as the fact that you've had no visible means of support for a year. Then there's the fact that you've never introduced Alison to any of your friends, presumably because she would be shocked. There's also the fact that you are a man who appreciates and uses money in rather large quantities. The evening clothes you're wearing are handmade and the Ferrari you drive has a custom-designed interior. Such things cost money, Mr. Drake. I think you're planning to use my sister to augment your cash flow and I won't allow it."

"You'll tell her the truth about my past if I get any closer to her, is that it?"

"That's it. I would prefer to handle this just between the two of us, however. Everyone, including yourself, will be able to avoid a great deal of unpleasant gossip and speculation if you'll go quietly out of Alison's life."

"But you're prepared to subject all of us to that kind of talk if I refuse?"

"I'll make the biggest scene you ever saw if you don't leave her alone," she agreed flatly. "Once she's aware of your past she'll be forced to give you up. She's very conscious of her social status. Marrying a gangster would be the last thing she'd be likely to do. It would ruin her socially."

"But if I can convince her to throw such considerations to the winds and take the risk of marrying me...?"

"Then, Mr. Drake, you will force me to play my last card. Has Alison told you yet that I have control of her money until she's twenty-five? When I myself turned twenty-five, I inherited responsibility for both my own inheritance and hers. In two more years she'll get full control of her own funds but until then I have power of attorney."

"And you'll use that power to make sure I don't get a penny of Alison's money, correct?"

"I'm glad to see we understand each other, Mr. Drake."

"Oh, I understand you very well, Cassie. One question, though."

"What's that?" A faint flicker of triumph began to burn inside her. She was winning! Justin Drake was being backed into a corner and something told Cassie he would soon abandon the field. It was incredible that she had actually pulled this off, she realized jubilantly, but it looked as if her scheme had worked!

"Why don't you go straight to your sister with all of your conclusions and 'facts'? Why not tell her what I am and let her throw me over?" he asked quietly.

"Because she'd hate me for it, even though she'd probably still give you up."

"You sound as if you know exactly how a woman reacts in such circumstances," he drawled. His dark eyes gleamed in the shadows and Cassie found herself wondering uneasily just how much in control of the situation she actually was. Unconsciously she wiped her wet palms on the skirt of the expensive designer dress, leaving a sad, damp ripple in the perfectly aligned pleats. Justin's gaze followed the small action and the gleam flared brighter behind his narrowed lids.

"I do." She shrugged, bitterness tingeing her words. "I was warned that my husband was nothing but a fortune hunter."

"But you went ahead and married him anyway?"

"Fortunately, my sister has more common sense than I did at that age."

"I have a hunch it's more likely that you're just a different sort of female altogether," he growled. "One more inclined to take risks, perhaps. Look at you standing here blackmailing me. Do you see Alison ever trying anything quite so dangerous?"

He was right, of course. Alison was far more conventional. Alison was also gentler, more in need of protection. All good reasons why she should marry someone like Mark Seaton.

"I don't think there's any point in discussing Alison, although if you know her so well, then you know she won't continue seeing you if you threaten to jeopardize her social life."

"And even if I could seduce her into overlooking

the little matter of my background, you'll cut off her money for the next two years, right?'' he confirmed wryly. She didn't like the way those dark eyes were watching her.

"That's right. Find someone else who can give you what you want, Mr. Drake. Leave my sister out of this. She could never handle you and you know it. You'd gobble her up for breakfast.''

"Dracula doesn't 'gobble,' Cassie. He sips politely.''

"From the throat,'' she concluded tightly.

"From the throat,'' he agreed.

"Do we understand each other?'' she pressed, her body rigid with tension as she waited the results of her first and only blackmailing attempt. God, she was nervous! She would be so glad to end this evening. If everything was resolved tonight, Cassie promised herself, she would leave this weekend for the retreat she had planned. She was going to need it!

"We understand each other, Cassie,'' Drake finally allowed in a tone that made her skin crawl. She realized abruptly that he was furious!

It was difficult to discern at first because he did so little to give away his emotions. But now there could be no mistaking the dark glitter of his eyes or the controlled tension in his stance. Cassie swallowed uneasily but held her ground. Alison's whole life was at stake. She would not back down now.

"I'll do it, Mr. Drake,'' she got out softly. "I'll do everything I said I would if you persist in trying to seduce my sister.''

"I believe you,'' he admitted coolly.

"Then will you agree to leave her alone?"

"You don't seem to leave me much choice."

"I want your word on the subject!" she finally hissed, infuriated by his laconic answers.

"The word of a vampire, Cassie?" The flickering, dangerous smile appeared again at the edge of his mouth. "The word of an ex-casino owner? A fortune hunter? What good would such a man's promise be?"

She glared at him in frustration. "Just tell me you'll leave her alone!"

He shrugged with casual grace. "I'll leave her alone."

Cassie frowned, realizing she was waiting for something. The sense of waiting for the other shoe to drop or a sword to fall was strong in the small alcove. Dracula wasn't the sort to slink off obediently into the shadows. Was he? This easily? Cassie was more than a little afraid of her rather easy victory. When he said nothing else, however, but merely continued to watch her with that glittering, implacable gaze, she fumbled around for an exit line.

"Well, since the matter is resolved," she began industriously, "I think I'll be on my way."

"Having snatched my prey from my grasp, you're going to make good your escape?" he taunted silkily.

Why was she pressing her luck by hanging around this damn alcove! Cassie picked up her pleated skirts and inclined her head once in a firm gesture of farewell. She never made it to the arched door.

"Not so fast," Justin murmured sardonically as his hand closed around her bare shoulder. He jolted her to a halt and spun her around to face him. "If you're going to take the risk of depriving me of my intended prey, you'll have to take the consequences, won't you?''

"What do you mean?'' she gasped, genuinely frightened now by the look on his face. Instinctively her hands came up to push against his chest. It was like trying to shove a hunk of granite. Cassie's head snapped up in fury and fear and several more tendrils of hair escaped.

Justin's mouth came down on hers before she fully realized his intent. The shock of it left her devoid of breath. Even if she had been capable of struggling, there would have been little opportunity. Drake held her with arms that chained her body tightly to his. His kiss was heavy, overpowering, darkly dominant. It was as if he were out to prove that there was at least one area in which she was helpless.

He drank from her mouth, not asking for any response except surrender. His hands curled into the pleats of the dress, seeking the feel of the soft flesh beneath the material. Cassie was aware of him from the top of her head to the soles of her feet. Every inch of her body was terrifyingly aware of him and her own physical helplessness. The will to dominate was so strong in him at this moment that she could feel the coils of it surrounding her, trapping her. For long moments she could only accept the assault, her stunned senses too unstable to function properly.

Then a new element was infused into his kiss. Sensuality; a dangerous, pulsating sensuality the likes of which she'd never known began to flow from his body into hers. It sent a wave of sheer panic through her bloodstream. The sudden shot of adrenaline gave her the strength to tear her mouth from his.

Mutely she stared up at him, her breath coming in shallow gasps, her nails digging deeply into the fabric of his black jacket as she tried to maintain some distance between them.

Justin looked down at her intently. "Are you afraid of me, lady?"

"No!" she denied frantically, realizing she was lying through her teeth. "But I don't like being manhandled!"

"I'm not melting," he pointed out, as if mildly interested by the phenomenon.

"What the hell does that mean?" she flared.

"I told you that I thought you could cause any man who got out of line to dissolve into a puddle, remember? But I seem to be immune to your weapons. I haven't melted. What do you suppose that means, Cassie?"

"It means you're not particularly human!" she shot back, outraged.

"Maybe. Maybe not. You're wise to be afraid of me, though."

"I am not afraid of you!"

"You should be," he informed her laconically. "In fact, if you had half the common sense your sister has, you would already be taking to your heels."

"Are you threatening me, Mr. Drake?" she bit out. Her arms were growing sore just from the effort of trying to brace herself away from him. She was trembling from anger and fear and she didn't like the reaction. She'd never experienced this kind of panic around any man before in her life!

"Yes, Cassie," he drawled, "I'm threatening you. You'd better run, lady; as far as you can, as fast as you can."

Two

Her retreat had been ignominious, to say the least.

Cassie was still castigating herself for her hasty withdrawal from the hotel alcove three days later as she drove from San Francisco up the starkly beautiful Northern California coastline. She had run, not walked, from Justin Drake's intimidating presence, telling herself that she'd done what she'd come to the party to do, but knowing she was in full flight.

There was nothing he could do to her, she reminded herself forcibly. He had done as she'd ordered. Cassie knew that the seduction of her sister had been halted because Alison had told her so.

"He said he was too old for me," Alison said with a sigh over coffee the day after her birthday party. "And I suppose he is," she concluded philosophically. "But he was rather interesting!"

Cassie studied her sister closely. "You don't sound as if your heart is broken."

"Well, I shall definitely miss him, but I have to admit he didn't quite fit in with the rest of my friends. He always seemed a little aloof somehow. Maybe it's because he was so much older than they were."

And a lot more ruthless, hard and cynical than your other friends, Cassie added silently, aware of the relief coursing through her. The blackmail scheme had worked. She hadn't been so sure it would when she'd fled the party.

"I think you're right, Alison. I don't believe Justin Drake would ever have fit in with your crowd." That much was the truth! How well did Dracula mingle? "I'm glad you're not depressed about Justin breaking off the relationship."

"These things happen," Alison said with a cheeriness that surprised Cassie. How could her sister be recovering so quickly from a relationship with a man like Justin Drake? "Mark called this morning," Alison continued.

"Did he?" Perhaps that was why Alison was recovering so easily! "What did he have to say? Did he apologize for his temper a couple of months ago?" Cassie was well aware that Mark had given his longtime girlfriend an ultimatum. He wanted to be the only man in Alison's life, not part of a string. At twenty-six Mark was beginning to develop his strength as a man. Privately Cassie thought the maturity provided the finishing touch to the personality of a man who had always been fun and charming.

"He said he'd heard I'd stopped seeing Justin and

wanted to know if I'd finished playing games." Alison grimaced wryly.

"What did you tell him?"

"I told him that if he'd stop flexing his male ego I might see him this Saturday." Alison grinned.

Cassie had left San Francisco satisfied that her sister's life was back on course. With that crisis resolved she had been free to leave for the long-awaited month by the sea. She wasn't really running away, she reminded herself as she drove her bright-red Ferrari along the winding coastal highway. This trip had been planned long in advance, at least a month before Justin Drake had appeared on the scene. And besides, she wasn't afraid of him! There was absolutely nothing he could do to her!

Cassie was reminding herself of that simple fact for the hundredth time when she became aware of the pinging under the sleek hood of the expensive car. Her brows came together in an irritated expression. The damn car was always giving her trouble. Why did people like Justin Drake drive Ferraris that ran like sleek, powerful jungle beasts while she was always having to deal with pings and carburetor protests and broken widgets?

It was just like everything else she tried to spend her money on. It didn't seem to want to belong to her. She had not been born to be rich, Cassie thought with a sigh. She just wasn't cut out for it and everything she owned seemed aware of that fact. The unbelievably expensive Swiss watch on her wrist didn't keep proper time, the hundred-dollar-an-ounce perfume she had put on this morning had already faded and the suede jacket she had put on over her white blouse had left little bits of itself all over the collar. Now the Ferrari was pinging.

Well it could damn well ping, she decided violently and stamped down hard on the accelerator. The beautiful car leaped forward and the pinging intensified. At least it didn't sound fatal yet. She only had fifty more miles to go.

The pinging served to take her mind off Justin Drake for the remaining fifty miles. By the time she had reached her destination, a sleepy little town near the Oregon border, the noise under the hood had become a loud, angry hiss.

"You know very well there's not going to be a Ferrari mechanic within a hundred miles of here," she lectured the protesting car as she guided it along the route outlined on the map she had received from the real estate agent. "So you can just stop complaining."

Slowing the car, she watched for the town's post office, which was to be her first landmark. At the corner she turned right and found the promised road, which led another few miles to a high bluff overlooking the sea. It was getting dark and Cassie wanted to find the house she had rented before night fell.

As soon as she left the main streets of the little town the houses became scattered and sparse. The few she passed seemed to crouch in the wind, gazing broodingly down at the crashing surf far below. The area was perfect for what she had in mind. If a woman couldn't discover her true creative potential amid all this desolate splendor, where could she discover it?

Cassie began watching for the house pictured in the photograph that lay on her lap. She slowed the car a little more, peering through the gnarled, windswept trees that lined the narrow road. In another twenty minutes it was going to be quite dark.

A few fat drops of rain hit the windshield and Cassie automatically switched on the wipers. Predictably enough they refused to function at first, but after Cassie punched the mechanism with her hand a couple of times they ground into action.

Everything around her began to look gray in color. The stormclouds rolling in off the ocean had picked up no tints of orange or red from the sun that had disappeared a few minutes earlier. The twisted pines on the cliffs couldn't really be described as green. They, too, were gray. The occasional weather-beaten house was also part of the monochromatic color scheme. The rain was obviously settling in for a long stay and soon it obscured most of the scenery. The candy-red hood of the Ferrari was the only bright spot in Cassie's field of vision.

She slowed the exotic car even further, anxiously watching for the turnoff that had been described by the real estate agent. She had climbed a good distance above the sea now and the road became even narrower and more convoluted. The headlights picked up no more than a few feet of roadway as the rain closed in more thickly. Perhaps she should turn back toward town, Cassie thought, and find a motel for the night.

The Ferrari's heater seemed to be malfunctioning. She kept setting it higher and higher in an effort to ward off the chill that lay over the landscape.

"Damn heater," she muttered feelingly. "Spend a fortune on a car and the heater doesn't work. Ah-hah!" The last exclamation was elicited by a brief glimpse of a towerlike structure off to the left. It disappeared back into the fog as quickly as it had appeared, but the sight of it was enough for Cassie. She'd found the house in the photograph. Hastily she began searching for a road that would lead toward the place.

In the end she almost overlooked it. The twin stone pillars that had originally marked the driveway entrance were almost entirely concealed by a clump of scraggly vines. The drive itself was unpaved, and shortly after she'd turned onto it Cassie realized that if the rain persisted throughout the night, it would be a quagmire by morning. Good thing she hadn't decided to stop at a motel.

From what little she could see of the three-story structure perched on the cliff, the house was as promised: a huge, eccentrically ornamented Gothic mansion complete with a tower, a porte cochere and a heavy, brooding atmosphere. According to the real estate agent, it had been built by a nineteenth-century lumber baron for his wife and daughter. The lumber baron had died at the turn of the century. The wife had lived a reclusive existence in the rambling structure until the early 1900s. After her death the place had apparently gone through a series of owners, none of whom ever retained the mansion for long. A few recent ones had modernized the plumbing and added electricity.

"Costs a lot to heat an old place like that," the

agent had explained, "and there are always a lot of repairs that need doing. People get tired of trying to keep up with the demands of an old Victorian mansion. It's really not in very good shape, from what I understand. Third floor was designed as a ballroom and is unfurnished."

"Should make a good place for painting," Cassie had said happily, picturing herself in a lofty, well-lit studio.

"Oh, you're a painter?"

"Possibly."

The agent hadn't been quite sure how to respond to that so he'd continued reciting the few other facts he had about the mansion on the cliff. "The furniture on the ground floor and the second level is quite old and hasn't been kept in repair. It will probably be dusty and somewhat rickety." He had glanced up from his notes, wondering if that had discouraged his client. "I'm sure I could find you a much more comfortable place on the coast, Miss Bond. Considering the amount of money you're prepared to spend for a month's residency, almost any of my owners would be more than happy to rent to you."

"No, no, this place sounds perfect. I want something with atmosphere. Tell me about the tower."

The agent had cleared his throat and gone back to his notes. "Other than the fact that it has one, I can't tell you too much about it. I've never actually seen the mansion, you realize. All I've got is some information the present owner supplied in a phone call. I believe he said that the tower had curving windows on the second level, however, and that there was a nice tiled room there.''

"Sounds perfect for writing."

The agent had frowned in confusion. ''You're a writer?''

"Maybe."

''I see. Well, there are several bedrooms on the second floor. The ground floor has the usual kitchen, library and parlors. It's quite a big place, you understand, Miss Bond. Huge, in fact. Are you sure you want to rent this much space?''

"Yes."

''And the owner didn't want to go to the expense of having it cleaned....''

"That's okay."

The agent had finally abandoned the task of trying to dissuade her. ''Very well, here's the rental agreement.'' Cassie had signed without any hesitation.

Now, in spite of the fog and rain, she was well pleased with her decision. Parking the car under the elegant porte cochere, she dug the house key out of her purse and climbed out to stand beneath the stone structure. She eyed the door ahead of her, head tilted to one side.

''You know,'' she remarked to the sulking Ferrari, ''all this place needs is Dracula opening the front door and the sense of atmosphere would be complete.'' Then her brows snapped together in irritation as she realized that she was visualizing Justin Drake standing in the carved doorway. Such images were more than a little disturbing on a night like this. Whatever had made her think of him?

* * *

Two hours behind Cassie, the man she thought of as Dracula was experiencing no problems at all with his Ferrari. Justin Drake drove through the gathering storm with the same casual skill he did almost everything else. His excellent reflexes responded to the rapidly changing road conditions with speed and efficiency, leaving his mind free to consider once again the course of action he had undertaken.

Cassandra Bond deserved what was going to happen to her, he told himself. Did she really think she could get away with blackmailing him? She had nerve, that was for sure, but she needed to be taught a lesson. People didn't corner Justin Drake and then proceed to issue orders the way Cassie had done, not without paying a price.

He thought of her as she had appeared the night of Alison's party, the golden-brown hair amusingly disheveled and the beautiful makeup smudged. The gown had been expensive but she had wiped her palms on it as if she had been wearing a pair of jeans. The memory made his mouth twist into its parody of a smile and his dark eyes narrowed fractionally.

Until he was introduced to Cassie, Justin would never have guessed she and Alison were related. Alison's blond hair was always in a perfect halo around her beautiful face, framing guileless blue eyes and a charming little nose. She wore her clothes and her breeding with grace and familiarity. Alison was a lovely creature who fitted into her wealthy social milieu perfectly. She was exactly what Justin had decided he wanted.

It was infuriating to have been deprived of his goal

by someone like Cassie. Cassie was far wealthier than
her sister and her money, Justin knew, had been
earned, not inherited. The money Cassie had inherited, Alison once confided, had disappeared along
with her sister's first husband. It was after he had left
that Cassie had discovered she had an incredible talent for playing the stock market. With an astuteness
that bordered on the uncanny, Cassie had apparently
recouped her fortune and added to it.

But somehow Cassie never managed to wear her
money with the ease of her sister. On the three occasions when Justin had met Cassie, her hair had always been in mild disarray. Once there had been a
distinct smudge on a silk blouse; on another occasion
she had been wearing tennis shoes along with a suit
that had clearly been designed in Paris. Somehow the
suit had become a bit rumpled, Justin remembered.
The twisted curve of his mouth became a little less
harsh for a moment as he summoned up the picture.

She had been scowling at him on all three occasions. The recollection of her contempt hardened his
expression once again. Cassie had realized from the
first instant that Justin Drake was not pursuing Alison
out of love.

It was more than infuriating to be so easily out-
maneuvered by the little wretch. It was downright hu-
miliating. She had pulled off that blackmail stunt with
unerring accuracy, zeroing in on his vulnerable point
with a skill that elicited his admiration even as it
made him furious. She had been quite right. Alison
would have refused to marry him if she had known
the truth about his past. Cassie hadn't even needed to

throw in the additional threat of cutting off her sister's money.

Justin's hands tightened briefly on the steering wheel. It was impossible not to appreciate Cassie Bond's courage and nerve even as he acknowledged his own angry response. She had cost him more than she knew, however, and he wasn't about to let her go unpunished.

In spite of her desire for "atmosphere," Cassie had a few distinct qualms as she walked through the old mansion and experimented with light switches. A few lamps worked, fortunately. Good thing she'd thought to bring along some extra light bulbs, however. Most of the bulbs beneath the dusty, torn shades were burned out.

Much of the parlor and library furniture was draped in dingy sheets in a halfhearted attempt to protect the various pieces. When she climbed the grand, carved staircase to the second level, however, Cassie discovered that no one had bothered to cover the upstairs furniture.

There were huge four-poster beds in the three bedrooms that had furniture. But when she struck the bumpy mattresses with the flat of her hand, dust rose in a musty cloud. It looked as though she'd have to spend the first day of her creative retreat clearing a few rooms in order to make them livable. Some creativity!

"I'm going to flip if it turns out my true talents lie in the realm of housekeeping!" she announced down-

stairs in what must have been the breakfast or morning room.

Her voice seemed unnaturally loud beneath the
thirteen-foot ceilings. It rang through the huge, silent
house. Far more unnatural and quite unnerving, however, was the response her words received. Cassie
jumped as a low, plaintive cry reached her ears.

Even as she reacted so abruptly, her common sense
identified the rasping cry. There was a cat in the
house. Curiously, Cassie walked across the hall into
the dining room. Dressed only in a pair of jeans and
a white shirt, she was beginning to feel very chilled.
The cat was probably cold, too. Cassie's loosely anchored bundle of hair shifted precariously to one side
of her head as she bent down to peer beneath the
magnificently carved sideboard.

"Hello, cat. Are you cold? Want to come with me
to build a fire in the library fireplace? The radiators
don't seem to be working very well."

The green-eyed monster under the sideboard regarded her unblinkingly. He was a truly mammoth
cat, Cassie realized, and his coat appeared to be solid
black. "You're quite perfect for this house, cat. Are
you sure you don't want to come out and meet me?
I'm harmless. What's more, I've got food!"

It struck Cassie in that moment that she was hungry
herself. Rising to her feet she went into the huge
kitchen and began investigating the bags of groceries
she had brought. Ten minutes later she had fixed two
very large tuna-fish sandwiches. Putting each one on
a paper plate, she carried them back into the dining
room. There she sat alone at the baronial dining table,

ensconced in the lord's chair, and ate her tuna sandwich. The other plate she left on the floor in front of the sideboard. It took exactly two and a half minutes before the big cat glided cautiously out to sample the tuna.

"You remind me of someone I recently met, cat. Lucky for you I know that Dracula's pets were always werewolves and not cats!" The animal ignored her, concentrating on the free handout with single-minded intensity. Cassie decided he was not truly wild, just wary of humans.

After the meal she located a stack of old wood on the porch behind the kitchen, some of which was fairly dry. The wind was beginning to pick up considerably now that darkness had fallen and the rain was coming down in heavier and heavier sheets. It was impossible to see more than a few feet beyond the porch.

"If I couldn't hear the sound of the surf at the bottom of the cliff, I wouldn't even know I was near the ocean!" she complained to the cat, who now sat curled on a chair in the library. The green eyes followed her every movement as she set about building a fire.

It was a struggle. Cassie hadn't built many fires. Her San Francisco townhouse had a lovely fireplace but it burned gas in the fake pile of logs, not real wood. She wound up using the grocery bags she had brought with her to start the blaze. Then she had to dig through the pile of wood on the back porch for a considerable length of time in order to find enough bits and pieces to use as kindling. The resulting blaze was not very satisfactory.

Cassie glowered at the little flickering flame, leaning forward on her knees to feed it carefully. The green-eyed cat continued to watch in aloof disapproval.

"You're free to leave anytime, cat. If you don't like the fire I've got going you may take yourself off to another room. Nobody's stopping you!"

The animal ignored the waspish tones and continued to watch dispassionately.

"Are you sure you don't have any vampire blood in you?"

An abrupt crack of lightning streaked through the nighttime sky, cutting off whatever answer the creature might have made. It was followed by a roll of thunder and the wind seemed to howl louder than ever.

"I pity anyone still out on that road tonight," Cassie muttered, half to herself and half to the cat. She moved a little closer to the fireplace. There was a dusty area rug on the hardwood floor, which she used as a cushion as she surveyed the draped furniture around her. The thought of going upstairs to the cold, dank bedrooms was not appealing. Tonight it seemed more inviting to sleep down here. After a few moments of intent contemplation Cassie got to her feet and began investigating the larger pieces of furniture.

The only item that looked even remotely usable as a bed was a velvet-covered sofa. Locating the quilt she had brought with her and the two soft pillows, Cassie contrived a bed of sorts. It was going to be cramped but she thought it might work. When the next crackle of lightning blazed outside the library's bay window Cassie irritably pulled the tall, heavy curtains. They were torn in a few places and definitely frayed, but at least they served to block out the disquieting effects of the lightning strikes.

"It's not that I'm scared of storms, cat, it's just that I wouldn't want the lightning to disturb your rest," she told the animal laconically. It was, in part, the truth. Normally she wasn't in the least alarmed by storms. But then she had never been through one while staying in a huge, empty mansion on a deserted cliff overlooking a storm-tossed sea.

"Atmosphere," she reminded herself aloud. "Atmosphere." Nothing could be farther from downtown San Francisco or the stock market, and getting away from both had been her goal.

She was still mumbling to herself about "atmosphere" when the lights went out.

Cassie came to a startled halt in front of the struggling fire. There was no hopeful flicker from the lamps around her, nothing to indicate the lights might come back on and stay. The mansion had been plunged into complete and utter darkness.

"Damn!"

This was carrying atmosphere a bit too far. Cassie crouched beside the small fire and cautiously fed the flame another bit of wood. The black cat remained where he was, coiled on a draped chair. His eyes still followed Cassie's every move.

"Candles, cat. We need candles. Maybe there are some in the kitchen." It was tricky finding her way back down the main hall to the kitchen at the rear of the old house, but Cassie eventually stumbled into it. By sense of touch she worked her way round the cupboards. Why hadn't she thought to bring a flashlight? She had the fifth drawer open when a bolt of lightning obligingly illuminated the inside.

"We're in luck, cat!" she called down the hall. "Not only candles but matches!" A few moments later she had illuminated the library with candlelight. The elegant candle holders on the mantel over the fireplace and on the ends of the glass bookcases were all soon filled.

"What do you think, cat? Is it romantic?"

The huge black cat blinked his eyes once and appeared to go to sleep.

"You're a lot of fun, you know that? I can't tell you how nice it is to have someone as chatty as yourself to pass the evening with!" Cassie opened her Vuitton suitcase and rummaged around inside. The long-sleeved, high-necked brushed-cotton nightgown she took out was far from being the most expensive piece of lingerie in her wardrobe, but it was definitely the most comfortable. And, like her jeans, it was content to be worn by her. It didn't make trouble, like the more luxurious clothing she owned.

She changed in front of the fire, wishing there were a little more heat to be had from the poor flame. It was going to be a long night. Cassie was just pulling the cotton nightgown over her head when she heard a demanding knock on the porte cochere door. The sound made her freeze.

Automatically she glanced across at the cat. He had

his eyes open now, staring out the door into the hall. The knock came again, heavy and commanding. The cat waited.

Cassie waited, too, filled with a strong premonition of danger. Not being the premonition-prone type, she discovered it was a new sensation. She didn't care for it. "Maybe it's a neighbor, cat. Someone who's come to check on us. Maybe it's the owner of this place. Wouldn't that be a thoughtful gesture, to come out in this storm to make sure the new tenant was all right?"

The cat swung his head around to eye her with a disgusted glance. Of course it wasn't the owner. The owner lived in town and nobody in his right mind would drive up the winding cliff road on a night like this. If the owner had cared about his tenant, he would have taken the time to have the place cleaned.

The knock came for a third time, carrying a summons Cassie realized she couldn't ignore. As if drawn by invisible strings she trailed down the hall toward the door, carrying a candle in her left hand. The cotton nightgown wafted out behind her as she padded barefoot along the parquet floor. The loose knot of her hair had given up in its attempt to stay in place and the golden-brown mass cascaded thickly to her shoulders. She was about to peer through the small pane of glass set in the middle of the massive door when something brushed around her bare ankles.

"What are you doing out here, cat?" she hissed softly. The animal ignored her. Sitting down, he wrapped his tail around his feet and looked up expectantly.

The knock came once more, conveying a demand that had to be confronted.

"Who is it?" she called out a little shakily as she tried to look through the clouded glass pane. All she could make out was the dark shape of a man.

"Justin Drake. Let me in, Cassie."

She straightened immediately, deeply startled. Justin Drake? Here on her doorstep? No wonder she'd had a premonition of danger. "Go away!"

"Don't be an idiot, Cassie. You know damn well I'm not going to go away. Open the door."

"Not on your life. Get out of here, Mr. Drake. I have no desire to see you again and you know it!"

"Cassie, there's no way on earth I can get back down that road tonight. What's left of it is like quicksand. Open the door."

"What are you doing here, anyway?" she shot back, vastly annoyed as well as very uneasy.

"Let me in and I'll tell you."

"No thanks."

"Cassie, the wind is blowing forty miles an hour out here. It's cold and it's wet and I've had a hell of a long drive."

"Tough."

"Cassie, if you don't let me in this minute, I'm going to break one of the windows and let myself in," he told her flatly.

He'd do it, too. Cassie was absolutely certain of it. In a huge house like this there would be no way she could guard each and every window. "Damn you, Justin Drake, if you so much as lay a finger on me

I'll call the sheriff!'' It was an empty threat. There was no telephone in the mansion.

"I'm not here to strangle you, Cassie, although the idea is tempting. Now open the door and stop cringing.''

It was the accusation of cringing that did it. Infuriated by it, Cassie flung open the door and stood glaring up at him. The wind caught her gown, plastering it against her body. The candle flame revealed the gleaming dark eyes of Dracula for an instant and then was snuffed out by the force of the gale that swept hungrily through the doorway.

The descent of complete darkness made Cassie gasp. Instinctively she stepped backward, aware of Justin's shadowed form moving into the hall. A second later she heard the front door slam shut.

"What the hell are you doing running around with only a candle? Lights go out?''

"You're very observant. Since you can probably see in the dark anyway, why are you worried about lights?'' she muttered. A loud screech of protest ricocheted through the hall.

"What the devil is that?'' Justin growled.

"The cat,'' she rasped, disgusted with the fact that the sudden cry had shaken her. Her nerves were falling apart, she thought distractedly. What was she doing standing in the hall of a lightless old mansion, talking to Dracula? "And I thought I wanted a little atmosphere,'' she grumbled, feeling her way along the wall toward the library. She could barely make out the few dancing shadows that indicated the fire was still alive. The cat brushed her leg again as he hurried on ahead of her to settle back into his chosen chair.

"You call that a fire?" Justin followed her into the room, moving with an uncanny silence that was distracting in itself.

"I quit Girl Scouts the second week, so I missed the seminar on building a fire," she mumbled caustically. "If you think you can do any better, go ahead."

Without another word he moved into the faint light thrown by the faltering flame and knelt to deal with the fire. "What in hell made you choose this crumbling monstrosity of a house as a place to hide, Cassie?"

"I am not hiding from you, Justin Drake!" She considered using a candlestick on his head. But attempted murder still seemed a bit extreme. He wouldn't really hurt her, would he?

"How did you find me, anyway?" she demanded.

"I asked Alison, of course," he replied succinctly, concentrating on his efforts to revive the fire.

"Why are you here, Justin?" she made herself ask calmly as she sank down on the velvet couch.

"I'm going to teach you a lesson, Cassie." He stoked the flames with efficient ease, creating a healthy blaze that illuminated his own hard profile.

Cassie went very still, real fear coursing down her spine as she stared at his kneeling figure. He was dressed in a black pullover sweater and a pair of black jeans. The black calfskin boots on his feet looked sinister.

Desperately she fought for some semblance of her

normal spirit. But trapped in a firelit room facing a man who looked right at home in a crumbling old mansion, she found it was difficult to sound cool and determined. ''I've warned you, Justin Drake, if you try to hurt me in any way...''

''Credit me with a little subtlety, Cassie. I'm not going to beat you.'' He rose lithely to his feet and turned to face her, the strange smile edging his mouth.

Cassie looked up at him warily, aware of feeling very chilled even though the room was rapidly warming at last. ''Exactly what kind of a threat are you making, Justin?'' she whispered tightly.

He closed the space between them, coming to a halt in front of her. Almost casually he reached down to capture her chin between his thumb and forefinger. His dark eyes glittered in the firelight, brilliant and unreadable.

''I told you to run, lady, remember? Well, you did run and now I've caught up with you. You never had a chance, you know? But now the chase is over. I'm going to teach you not to look at me as if I'm not worthy of you. I'm going to change your attitude completely, in fact.''

''What are you talking about?'' she whispered, immobilized by the heavy power in him. Cassie felt as if she were under a spell.

''I'm going to seduce you, Cassandra Bond. You're going to compensate me in bed for what I lost when I gave in to your threat of blackmail.''

Three

Cassie's reaction was immediate and electric. "Not a chance," she whispered fiercely. She dodged free of his hand, leaping to her feet and moving to put the sofa between them. "I would no more go to bed with you than I would with...with..."

"With Dracula?" he asked, making no effort to drag her out from behind the sofa.

"Yes, damn it!"

"As I recall, Dracula got any woman he wanted." His dark eyes gleamed with wicked humor.

"Well, you haven't got that kind of track record, have you? You didn't get my sister and you're not going to get me!" she gritted, aware of feeling far too vulnerable in the cotton nightgown. "Now, if it's money you want..."

"You're still willing to pay me off? How generous of you," he drawled.

She eyed him suspiciously. "Go away and I'll send you a check."

He shook his head. "It won't work, Cassie. I don't want your money."

"You can't possibly want me, either!"

"I'll admit you're different from your sister," he acknowledged, surveying the picture she made in the old-fashioned nightgown.

"So why bother trying to rape me if you don't find me attractive?" she snapped.

"I didn't say I was going to rape you. I said I was going to seduce you."

"I don't see much difference," she gasped.

"There's a world of difference," he said gently. "Raping you wouldn't change the way you look at me, would it? There would just be more contempt and disdain than ever in those golden eyes."

"Plus sheer hatred!"

His mouth twisted wryly. "Yes. And I don't want you to hate me, Cassie. I want you to desire me. I want you in the palm of my hand. I want you looking at me with eyes full of passion and need. I want you to surrender completely. Now do you understand? That's going to be your punishment for crossing me."

Cassie could hardly breathe. She longed to run and knew that was impossible. As she stared at him another bolt of lightning crossed the sky, a bolt so brilliant that it was visible even through the rips in the old curtains. The thunder followed almost at once. Across the room the black cat watched Cassie with eyes as unreadable as Justin's. Cassie felt trapped with not one but two sources of menace.

"Justin," she began shakily and was horrified by the pleading note in her voice. Desperately she strove to control it and tried to reason with him. "Justin, I had to stop you from marrying my sister. Don't you see? You would have been all wrong for her. She's a creature of the daylight, full of laughter and fun. She's made for the world she lives in; beautiful and charming and vivacious. She deserves someone like her. What's more, she deserves someone who genuinely loves her. You don't love her. You just wanted to use her!"

"I don't think there's any point in discussing your sister," he said harshly. "And I'm well aware that you think I'm her opposite in every way. I'm a creature of the night in your eyes, aren't I? I'm not full of laughter and fun. I'm not handsome and I seriously doubt that you find me charming. It's true, I didn't love her. But then love is a myth, so I don't see that it matters. In any event, it's all behind us. I know Alison well enough to realize she wouldn't marry me if you told her what you know of my past. She wasn't exactly in the throes of an undying passion for me, you see. I rather think that in her own way she was using me herself."

"That's ridiculous! Alison doesn't use people."

"No?" He lifted one shoulder in a shrug. "I'll reserve judgment on that. But none of that affects us tonight, does it? The game has moved to the next stage. You got in my way, Cassie Bond. You deprived me of something I wanted, so you're going to give me something in return. And in the process you're going to learn a lesson about treating me as if I were dirt.''

"But I never meant…that is, I didn't treat you that way," she sputtered. "I was only trying to protect Alison!"

"You succeeded in saving your sister from my clutches," he taunted, "but I don't think there's much you can do to save yourself."

"What makes you think you can seduce me!" Cassie ground out furiously.

"Instinct," he said succinctly.

"Instinct!"

"Umm. It has something to do with the way you reacted when I kissed you in that hotel alcove, and—"

"I didn't react to you," she interrupted quickly.

"And something to do with the way you look at me," he continued ruthlessly. "You challenge me, Cassie, and when a woman challenges a man, she's usually vulnerable to him."

"That's perfectly idiotic psychology!"

"We'll find out, won't we? Now, where are the flashlights?" He seemed to have grown bored with the conversation and glanced around the room consideringly.

"I don't have a flashlight," she replied testily, half-relieved he was going on to another topic and half-enraged that he could talk of seducing her and then forget the matter so quickly. Justin Drake was unlike any man she had ever met, she realized in dismay. The normal rules for handling men didn't seem to apply to him. But he did build a nice, comforting fire.

"What do you mean, you don't have a flashlight? Didn't you have one in your car?"

"No."

"You really came prepared, didn't you?" He stalked over to a huge mahogany desk and absently opened a few drawers.

"I came up here to find myself, not a flashlight!"

He looked at her oddly. "To find yourself?"

"Never mind," she muttered, moving out from behind the sofa to edge closer to the warmth of the fire. Cautiously she put out her hands to the blaze. "Just forget the flashlight. I don't have one and it would be difficult to search the house tonight in the dark. I was lucky to locate some candles in the kitchen!"

"I'll get mine from the car," he announced deliberately and walked out into the hall without a backward glance. The front door opened and closed.

Cassie watched him go and then mumbled gruffly to the cat. "Figures he'd be prepared, doesn't it, cat? He probably stuck a flashlight in his car this afternoon just so he could produce it under the right circumstances and make me look silly for being unprepared."

The cat said nothing, merely continuing to watch her with slitted green eyes. If ever a creature had looked genuinely evil, Cassie decided, it was that cat. "I'm beginning to regret feeding you that tuna sandwich," she informed him.

"What tuna sandwich?" Justin asked as he paced back into the library, flashlight in hand.

"I made that damn cat and myself a tuna sandwich earlier," she explained shortly.

"Aren't you going to offer me one?" One black brow arched inquiringly as he knelt to feed another log to the cheery fire.

"I would have thought you preferred a more liquid diet," she observed sarcastically.

"Well, I'd be glad of a glass of wine, too, of course, if you've got it."

"That's not what I meant," she grumbled, giving him plenty of room near the hearth. It made her very uneasy to be near him but the lure of the fire was too great to ignore.

"I see. I've got news for you, Cassie: whatever I might prefer to drink, I also like solid food. Will you fix me a sandwich?"

She slanted him a savage glance. "Why on earth should I go out of my way to fix you anything at all?"

"You fed the cat," he pointed out innocently.

"And I'm already beginning to regret it. Look at that monster. I think he's probably some witch's familiar!"

"It's just a cat, Cassie." Justin sighed. Then he gave her his flickering smile. "And I'm just a man."

"Uh-huh."

"You are scared of me, aren't you?" He sounded quite satisfied.

"No, I am not scared of you! I am furious with you, outraged by your assumptions and by your behavior, but I am not afraid of you!" She held herself proudly as she made the declaration, telling herself privately that the words were not a complete lie.

"Good." He straightened, flashlight in hand.

"Then let's go make me a tuna sandwich, hmm? I'm hungry. Who knows what I might do if I'm not fed?" He deliberately glanced at her throat and Cassie would have kicked him if she hadn't been barefoot.

"The food is in the kitchen. The refrigerator was working before the electricity went off. Look in there." She gazed fixedly at the fire, refusing to give any more ground. The casual way he was taking control was frightening in itself. She must resist the small aggressions or she would be helpless in the face of the more serious ones. *My God!* she thought suddenly, realizing the direction of her thoughts. *Does that mean I really am vulnerable in some way?*

"Come with me, Cassie," he ordered softly, too softly. "I want you to fix me a sandwich."

He made no move to touch her, facing her in front of the hearth with a calm, implacable expression. The firelight danced on his arrogant features and Cassie shivered. She fought the small battle with silent willpower but she knew she was going to lose. She wasn't certain exactly why but she knew it would be so. The only thing she could do was try to salvage some pride from the scene.

"I suppose," she began imperiously, "that since you built me a decent fire, I can fix you a sandwich!" Spinning around on her bare heel she grabbed a candlestick off the nearest shelf and started down the hall toward the old kitchen. Justin didn't say a word as he followed her, but she could feel the intense satisfaction in him. He used his flashlight to augment the candle flame.

"You look a little supernatural yourself, in that old-fashioned gown and with your hair tumbling down around your shoulders,'' he mused as he watched her slap together a hasty tuna sandwich. ''A man could be excused for thinking he'd encountered a ghost if he saw you the way I did when you opened the door tonight. You look very...*interesting,* by candlelight, Cassie.''

She glared at him briefly. ''If you're trying to seduce me, you're supposed to say I look beautiful by candlelight. Not just interesting.''

He didn't respond for a moment and then he said quietly, ''I'm beginning to think 'interesting' is a lot more attractive in the long run than 'beautiful.'''

''What in the world does that mean?'' she scoffed, slamming a slice of bread down on top of the tuna fish and handing him the uncut sandwich.

He took the sandwich without protest and shepherded her back down the hall. ''I'm not sure yet. I'm working on it. I'll let you know when I figure it out.''

''Never mind,'' she gritted, hurrying back toward the fire in the library. ''We have another problem on our hands at the moment. There are three bedrooms upstairs with beds in them. Help yourself.''

''Where are you going to sleep?''

She flinched. ''Down here. On that little sofa. As you can see, there is definitely not room for two.''

He ignored that. ''What's wrong with the bedrooms? Too cold?''

''Among other things.''

''Haunted?'' he murmured dryly.

''Of course not. But the beds are dusty and need

to be aired, so I decided to sleep in front of the fire tonight.''

"Sounds like a good idea.''

"I've told you, there isn't room for two on that sofa and I certainly don't intend to give it up to you!'' she shot back, not looking at him.

"I'll make up a bed on the floor. There must be some salvageable pillows and blankets upstairs. In a few minutes I'll go up and have a look.'' And to Cassie's distress, he looked quite pleased with the way things were turning out.

Cassie awoke the next morning to silence and the sensation of a heavy weight on her stomach. She opened her eyes to find the ebony cat sound asleep on her midsection and Justin standing over her with a steaming cup in his hand. There was amusement in the depths of his eyes as he watched her take in the scene.

"The storm has passed and the electricity has been restored,'' he said. "I found the instant coffee you brought with you.'' He was wearing a khaki shirt with his jeans this morning. A pleasant change from black, Cassie decided. But it didn't lessen the overall impression of compelling masculine power, she realized dazedly.

"Would you mind getting this cat off me?'' she managed to ask crisply, struggling to sit up. The cat appeared unaware of her efforts and merely shifted himself to a more comfortable position in her lap.

"I think he likes you.''

"Impossible. I have the feeling this cat is incapable

of liking anyone. He just uses people. He was probably cold last night so he thought he'd use me to keep warm.''

''Not a bad idea,'' Justin said mildly, handing her the cup of coffee as she shot him a quelling glance. ''I wouldn't have minded using you for the same purpose myself.''

''Not a chance.'' Cassie sipped the coffee cautiously. ''In fact, Justin, I have given our situation some serious thought,'' she announced boldly.

''Have you?'' He sat down in a nearby chair and watched her with interest. ''What conclusions have you reached?''

''You're going to have to leave. Today. Justin, I mean it. This place is mine for a month. If you don't go willingly, I shall have the local sheriff throw you out. Very embarrassing for you, I'm sure. One way or another, I want it clear that you're not staying here to stage your grand seduction.''

''Aren't you even curious to see whether or not you can be seduced against your will?''

''I already know the answer and the answer is 'no'!''

''Then why be in such a hurry to toss me out?''

''Because I don't want you here!'' she seethed. ''And I don't think I want this dumb cat here, either. He reminds me of you!'' She plucked the limp, heavy bundle off her lap and set it down on the floor. The cat immediately sat down on his haunches and began cleaning his fur just as if he'd jumped down from her lap on his own accord.

''I'm going to stay, Cassie.'' It wasn't a threat exactly, just a simple statement of fact, which made it all the more threatening.

Cassie watched him for a long moment. "Then I'll have to go and get the sheriff," she finally stated defiantly.

"I'll talk myself out of any scene you try to create." He shrugged. "Go ahead, if you want, but it won't work. You'll only come off looking like a petulant lover in the midst of a quarrel. I guarantee I can make you look the part in front of a sheriff or anyone else. You're the one who will be humiliated."

He meant it, she realized helplessly. And he could probably do just as he said. What options did that leave her?

"You could try running again," he suggested, as if he'd just read her mind.

"I didn't run the first time! This trip has been scheduled for the past three months!"

"If you do choose to run again, I'll come after you. I've got all the time in the world, Cassie. I'll use whatever it takes."

"Meaning you don't have a real job?" she gritted.

"No more than you do," he agreed easily.

Frustrated and furious, Cassie tossed back the quilt and leaped off the sofa. "One of us is going to leave today, Justin, and I intend to see that it's you!" She marched out of the library and upstairs to the second floor, where she had discovered a bathroom with plumbing that worked. As she left the room, she was aware that he followed her with his eyes, eyes that were dark and gleaming and full of lethal intent.

Lethal? The word stuck in her mind as she hurriedly dressed in jeans and a red sweater. Surely not! Lethal meant deadly. She hadn't really intended to use that word. Justin was out to punish her, not kill her. His past was shady but there was no hint of his resorting to murder to settle his problems! Her imagination was really in high gear here in this old place, she thought grimly. Atmosphere. Too much of it.

She walked bravely into the kitchen a few minutes later to find Justin rummaging around in her grocery sacks. He was obviously making himself right at home.

"What did you bring for breakfast?" he asked conversationally.

"Only enough for myself," she returned sweetly.

"You're in a cheery mood this morning," he drawled, locating a box of cereal.

"I'm surprised you're even awake!" she muttered, stalking across to the refrigerator.

"I'm a very advanced sort of vampire," he growled. "I've learned to endure the light of day. Don't even have to drag my coffin full of dirt around with me anymore."

She considered that as she pulled out a carton of milk. "Was it something of an adjustment, giving up the night world of casino gambling to become a day person?"

"Like I said," he returned laconically, "I've learned to endure the light of day." He leaned against the counter, his arms folded across his chest. "Come to think of it, though, this is the first time you've actually seen me in broad daylight, isn't it? It seems like every time we've met, it's been at night. Do I look any less sinister to you now in sunlight?''

"No."

"Good. I wouldn't want to think I'm losing my natural charm. Want some more coffee?"

"Yes, please. I didn't sleep very well last night.''

"I know. Spent most of the night waiting to see if you'd have to defend yourself, didn't you?'' He put the kettle on the old electric stove. "Why in the world did you pick this old house for a vacation spot? There must have been lots of more modern places you could have rented. What are you planning to do here, Cassie?''

"Whatever I feel like doing. Whatever I feel *inspired* to do, I should say,'' she told him honestly. "This month of experimentation is very important to me, Justin. I don't want you spoiling it for me. Do you understand?''

"Having an affair with Dracula should be fairly experimental. Why not give it a try?''

"Don't be ridiculous.''

"You know, other than your sharp tongue, you're kind of cute in the mornings. All fresh and alive-looking. A day person, hmm?''

"Definitely.'' She plunked the milk carton down on the counter and grudgingly filled two cereal bowls from the box of granola she had brought with her. "We can take these into the dining room,'' she allowed in resignation. Damn it, there had to be a way to evict Justin Drake! In the light of a new day she ought to be able to find it.

"What is it you're going to experiment with?'' he

asked, following behind her with his long, silent stride as she headed for the magnificent old dining room.

"This and that." Her mind was too involved with the immediate problem of getting rid of him to pay much attention to the question.

"That sounds rather mysterious," he observed, sitting down at one end of the huge oak table.

Cassie deliberately sat down at the far end, putting as much distance between them as possible. "There's nothing mysterious about it! I'm here to discover my true creative potential. What are you laughing at?" she added irritably. She could actually see laughter in his eyes. It was odd to see real emotion there, any kind of emotion. He usually looked so cold and aloof.

"Nothing, really. It's just that you look rather amusing sitting in that huge chair with your hair in that crazy little topknot."

Instantly Cassie lifted her hand to feel the knot of hair. It was already coming loose, as usual. She frowned severely and went back to munching cereal.

"I like you better without that eye makeup and odd lipstick you were wearing the night of the party," Justin went on smoothly. "Jeans and a sweater sort of suit you."

"Look, Justin, if this is your idea of a seductive conversation, I've got news for you. I know damn well how I appear when I'm dressed for a party and I know how I look in jeans. Believe me, I'm not thrilled with the fact that I can't wear beautiful, sophisticated clothes very well. Telling me jeans and a sweater 'sort of suit me' is not going to make any points!"

"Okay, how about if I compliment you on what I hear is your phenomenal ability in the stock market? Your sister tells me you've got the Midas touch."

"I find the subject distinctly boring."

"Making money is boring?" He sounded genuinely surprised.

"Making money in the stock market is. For me at any rate. I've got all the money I could possibly use and what good does it do me? My Ferrari pings, my four-thousand-dollar Swiss watch doesn't work, I get runs in my Dior stockings and I look funny in designer dresses! I wasn't made to be rich and live a sophisticated kind of life the way Alison does. I was made for something else. I'm thirty years old, Justin. I'm going to find out what I was really cut out to do in this world." Cassie flushed as she realized how she'd let herself be goaded into the intense little speech. Deliberately she shrugged as he stared at her. "Now you know what I'm doing here."

"This is where you're going to find your...uh, potential?" he asked carefully.

"My true creative potential." Excitement at the prospect of what lay ahead of her during the next month seized Cassie. She waved her cereal spoon in an energetic arc. Leaning forward intently, she told Justin. "I'm going to explore my abilities in art and poetry and writing. I feel certain I have some talent in one of those directions. All I need to do is open myself up during the next few weeks and *explore!* I'm going to let the real *me* come through. I needed a place with atmosphere. A romantic, moody background to help release the inner creative drive. You can't do that very well in a city, you see. I read this book a couple of months ago that says you have to remove yourself from the stifling, imprisoning forces around you and catapult yourself into a totally new environment if you want to free your inner self.'' She sat back in defiant triumph.

Justin looked at her as if totally fascinated. "Amazing,'' he finally said very dryly.

Cassie plunged back into her cereal. ''You can see why I really don't want to take the time to get myself seduced,'' she said caustically. ''I have much more important things to do while I'm here. Leave, Justin. Get in your car and leave me alone!''

"How could I possibly walk out now? I want to stick around and explore your creative potential with you. I can't wait to see the results,'' he said with suspicious politeness. Then he surprised her by adding, ''I think I'll take a walk on the beach below the cliffs after breakfast. A beach after a storm is an interesting experience. Will you join me?''

"No, thank you,'' she retorted stiffly. Actually, she would have loved to go down to the beach, but there was no way on earth she'd go with him.

To Cassie's amazement, Justin didn't try to force her to accompany him. He left the house a few minutes later and she breathed a sigh of relief as his disturbing presence was temporarily removed.

Then she began to pace through the house. Restlessly she went from room to room, taking another look at what she had rented. But all the while her mind was focusing on the problem presented by a vengeful Justin Drake. The man was dangerous. What

was she going to do? Run? She could take the car
and leave, of course. He'd have a tough time finding
her if she didn't tell anyone where she was going.

But it was annoying to be driven away from this
place. For months she had been studying and reading
as much as possible on creativity and how to release
the powers in the so-called right side of the brain.
Damn it, why should she be forced to hide from Justin?

Her face in an intent expression, she opened and
shut doors, examined closets and surveyed the bedroom situation. Then she returned downstairs and
went once more through the ground floor rooms. It
was on her last trip to the kitchen that she noticed a
door she hadn't seen before. It was situated in the hall
and was concealed when the kitchen door stood open.
The hidden door was massive and thickly paneled.

Curious, she opened the door and found herself
peering down a flight of steps that led into complete
darkness. The cat appeared at her ankle just as she
was considering whether or not to investigate the
room at the bottom of the steps.

"Oh, are you still around?" she asked. "I was hoping you'd left. Maybe when Justin goes, he'll take
you with him."

The cat looked up at her with his evil expression
but said nothing.

"I don't see a light switch. Wait a minute...no, it's
just a chunk of wood hammered onto the wall.
Wouldn't you think someone would have put a switch
here? Definite drawbacks to old, decrepit mansions,
cat. Maybe it's farther down on the wall."

Cautiously Cassie started down the steps, feeling along the wall for a light switch. The steps must lead down to an old basement, she decided. All sorts of interesting things might be stashed in the basement of an old house like this. Excited by the prospect, Cassie edged down one more step. In the dim light that filtered through the open door above her she couldn't make out more than a few steps.

"If you were a useful type of cat you'd run fetch me Justin's flashlight," Cassie called up to the huge creature framed in the doorway. This time the cat meowed and then sat silently.

"Why couldn't you have been a nice dog or something?" Cassie mumbled. "I like dogs. Some of my best friends are dogs. I— Oh, no!"

The exclamation came as the door above her suddenly swung shut. Instantly Cassie was plunged into darkness. "Damn," she muttered, feeling very alone all of a sudden. She hadn't heard the cat screech, so the slamming door must not have caught its tail.

Funny how an old basement had a distinct odor to it. The darkness around her felt damp and chilled. There was no handrail on the stair. Turning cautiously on the step, Cassie started back up to the closed door.

She reached it a moment later and found it locked.

"Of all the stupid, idiotic things. Why didn't I check the lock on the other side before I started down?" she wondered aloud. She stood on the top step, unconsciously rubbing her arms briskly. She could see nothing. Justin wasn't back from the beach yet so there was nothing to do but wait until she heard his step in the hall. If she could hear anything at all through that rather solid door, she added silently. Well, in a few minutes she'd start pounding.

What if he didn't respond?

Of course he'd respond, she assured herself in the next breath. However, it wouldn't hurt to continue her search for the light switch. A little light would be very welcome in this dungeon of a basement.

Feeling her way with her toes and keeping her hand on the wall beside her, Cassie started back down the steps. She stayed close to the walled side because the other was open. There was a sheer drop from the far edge of the steps to the basement floor below and Cassie was not in a mood for diving into unknown waters.

Nothing materialized beneath her hand. Just one more step or two, she promised herself firmly. Maybe the electrician who had wired the place had put the switch in the middle of the staircase.

She was trying to convince herself of that possibility when the step she had just reached gave way beneath her.

There was no warning, no creaking of wood, no feeling of instability prior to that instant. She simply found herself stepping down onto a surface that immediately collapsed beneath her weight.

With a scream she wasn't even aware of making, Cassie lost her balance and pitched sideways over the unrailed staircase.

Four

Cassie's next sensation was that of being suspended in midair. The strain in her hands was incredible. It took her a dazed moment or two to realize she had actually managed to catch hold of a stair tread as she'd fallen sideways. Now she hung there, clinging desperately to the edge of the stairs. Her legs dangled in black emptiness and she was vividly aware of a burning pain in one of them.

She was too stunned to even summon up a good scream, she realized vaguely. What was below her feet? Was it only a short drop to the floor of the basement or was it much farther? If she let herself go, would she fall on a barren surface or into a heap of nail-studded boards, garbage or rats?

Atmosphere. The damn place sure had atmosphere!

When would Justin return from his walk on the beach? If she'd had the sense to go with him she would not now be hanging by her fingernails over an abyss! Pain was building in her fingers, reaching to the muscles of her wrists and forearms. Cassie knew she wasn't going to be able to hang on for long. She had to find the strength to pull herself back up onto the stairs. If she could just get her leg up on a lower tread...

Why did her left leg hurt so much? She must have scraped it on the splintered edge of the staircase. Too bad she'd never mastered the art of chinning herself. But back in high school it was tough to figure out which skills you were going to need later on in life. In high school the only truly important abilities had appeared to be those that got you onto the cheerleading squad. Cassie remembered she hadn't mastered those, either.

What was she doing reminiscing about four of the worst years of her life? Grimly Cassie tried to swing her aching left leg up onto a lower tread. Her breath left her lungs in a near silent cry of agony as a new wave of pain shot through it. God, she must have really done some damage earlier.

Gasping for breath and willing herself to force back the pain so that she could think, Cassie hung by her hands another moment while she tried to analyze her situation. There was still no sound of anyone else in the house. When would Justin return?

What if he already had returned?

What if *he* had been the one who had closed the door at the top of the stairs?

No, that was ridiculous. What possible motive could he have to trap her in a basement? And how could he have known that the stairs were in such poor condition? The heavy door could easily have swung shut on its own.

Even as the questions raced through her brain, unpleasant answers suggested themselves. There in the total darkness it was easy to let her imagination take hold. It occurred to Cassie that Justin might have more than seduction in mind. It would be very convenient if she were out of the way. Not only would he then be free to go back to the plans he had made with Alison, but Alison herself would abruptly be a much richer prize. She would inherit all of Cassie's money.

It was crazy, Cassie assured herself. She was letting her fear and her pain make her think irrationally. First things first. She had to find her way down from her precarious position or risk dropping into the unknown below.

If she couldn't swing herself back onto the stairs, then she would have to try working her way down with her hands. Drawing a deep breath, she inched her left hand along the tread to which she was clinging until she found the short drop to the next lower step.

It was painful and it was risky but there weren't a lot of alternatives, Cassie forcibly reminded herself. How much farther could it be to a point where her feet would touch the floor? How deep were old basements? Surely not too deep? If only she could see!

The strain in her hands was rapidly becoming almost intolerable. Except that there was no option but to tolerate it. Slowly Cassie inched her way along until she felt another lower step. Where was Justin?

She halted her progress as the faintest of cries filtered through the door at the top of the stairs. The cat? Cassie decided she wasn't feeling terribly charitable toward the creature. For all she knew he might have casually leaned against the door himself! She wouldn't put it past him.

She bit her lip in agony as the pain in her hands built higher and higher. How much farther? A step at a time, she reminded herself. Literally, a step at a time. She worked her way down another one. If only her left leg didn't hurt so much. It wasn't going to hold her weight if she was forced to let go of her grip on the stairs, that was certain.

She had managed to ease her way down one more step when there was another sound behind the door at the top of the stairs. She glanced up automatically, even though she could see nothing. An instant later the door was flung open and Cassie was blinking up at Justin's dark form. He stood there, outlined against the daylight in the hall, and for a terrible moment Cassie wondered if he'd come to finish the job.

"Cassie?" A flashlight's beam cut a swath through the darkness. Her name was called again in a harsh, rigidly controlled voice that contained anger and something else, something Cassie couldn't identify.

"Hanging by a thread, Justin," she managed with what she thought was commendable nonchalance under the circumstances. She couldn't read the expression on his shadowed face. A second later the flashlight found her.

He swore incredulously and then started down the stairs. "Damn it, Cassie, what the hell are you doing?"

"Stirring the creative juices," she gasped. "Nothing like the atmosphere of an old basement, you know. Better watch that next step, Justin. It's a bit tricky."

He halted abruptly as his flashlight picked out the missing stair tread. She heard another expletive ground out from between clenched teeth and then he was carefully making his way past the gap.

"Hang on, Cassie. I'll be there in a minute."

"I'm looking forward to your arrival," she muttered laconically. He didn't sound as if he intended to step on her fingers when he reached her, she told herself bracingly. Surely a man like Justin Drake wouldn't play sadistic games with an intended victim. He'd simply complete the ugly business and not offer false hope. Wouldn't he?

Of course, he had wanted revenge, she reminded herself as he carefully tested each step. The flashlight beam was focused on the staircase and although some light now came from the open door she couldn't begin to see Justin's face.

"Justin?" This time there was no false bravado in her voice. She waited helplessly, knowing she was trapped.

"It's okay, Cassie. I've got you." He knelt on the step and set down the flashlight. Then he caught her wrists and began to pull her up as easily as if she'd only weighed a couple of pounds.

Cassie felt the sure strength in his arms and knew

he wasn't going to drop her. "Oh, Justin," she murmured, "I hurt so much."

"I have you, Cassie, you're safe now." His voice was husky and strangely reassuring as he drew her up beside him.

"My leg, Justin, I don't think I can stand on it." Her cramped fingers continued to ache even though she was no longer using them to support her whole body. She couldn't seem to uncurl them. Cassie swallowed against the pain.

Justin muttered something savage and the next moment he had Cassie in his arms, cradled against his chest. He started back up the stairs, careful to avoid the step that had broken beneath Cassie. When they reached the door, the cat was waiting for them. He followed as Justin strode down the hall to the library with his burden.

"What the hell? Cassie, your leg is bleeding. You really did a number on it, didn't you?" Justin's face was a grim mask as he set Cassie down on the sofa and rolled up the denim fabric of her jeans. "Damn it, woman, what were you doing on that staircase? If that cat hadn't been sitting by the door..."

"I just wanted to see what was down in the basement," she said in defense of herself, drawing in her breath sharply as he examined her leg. A long, shallow-looking slash extended for several inches down her calf. The blood still oozed freely from it.

"Here." Justin took one of her aching palms and placed it over the gash. "Press as hard as you can on it while I go get the emergency kit out of my car." He rose to his feet, looking thoroughly annoyed.

"Just wanted to see what was in the basement," he repeated sarcastically. "And you didn't even have a flashlight. Of all the idiotic, crazy things to do! Don't you realize the wood in an old house like this is often rotted?"

"I wonder if we could save the lecture until you get my leg bandaged?" Cassie glowered up at him, knowing there was undoubtedly pain as well as defensiveness in her eyes. She didn't need him to tell her she had been foolish.

Justin hesitated and then walked out of the library without a word, returning shortly with a small medical kit. He proceeded to carry Cassie into the kitchen, sitting her on the counter and adjusting her so that the injured leg extended into the sink. She watched stoically as he thoroughly washed her leg under running water and then prepared to dab the gash with antiseptic.

"This is going to hurt," he warned.

"Here, let me put it on, then. I can control it better that way." Cassie tried to remove the bottle from his hand but he refused to let her have it.

"I'll do it." Deliberately he applied the stuff in a quick, merciless fashion.

"Damn it! That hurts!" Cassie jumped, trying to pull her leg out of the way. "Justin, that's my leg, I'll take care of it!"

"It's over with," he announced, setting the bottle down on the counter. "Believe me, it's easier to get it done in a hurry than to stretch it out. It's like pulling off a Band-Aid. One quick yank is easier in the long run than pulling it off centimeter by centimeter."

She gave him a fulminating glance. "You have your medical theories and I have mine. I prefer my own methods."

"Meaning you're the type who pulls off the Band-Aid centimeter by centimeter?"

"Exactly. And I dab my antiseptic on slowly. In future, kindly remember that I prefer to do things my way!"

"We've got a small problem, then, haven't we?" He smiled laconically as he bandaged the leg and scooped her up off the counter. "I like to do things my way, also."

Cassie let that one pass, not feeling up to a full-scale argument over something as trivial as Band-Aids. She was silent as he carried her back down the hall to the sofa. It was only when he had released her that she commented blandly, "I noticed you didn't get too upset at the sight of blood."

He stood looking down at her. "I could hardly afford to be squeamish, could I? It would interfere with my career."

Was that a teasing light she saw in the dark gaze? Probably not. Dracula was not noted for his sense of humor. She watched as he moved over to the fireplace and began to restoke the blaze he'd created before his walk on the beach. The room was pleasantly warm, reminding her of just how chilled the basement had been.

"How do you feel?" Justin finished with the fire and stood up to lean casually against the mantel. His gaze swept her reclining figure.

Cassie stifled a groan. She knew she must look

more mussed than usual after the adventure in the basement. She didn't have to put her hand to her hair to know it was in a tangle. Her jeans were torn and her sweater was dirty.

"Not at my best, now that you mention it."

Justin nodded. "Well, that makes things easier, doesn't it?"

She blinked uncomprehendingly. "I beg your pardon?"

"It makes everything easier for you. This way you don't have to feel bad for not being able to toss me out of the house. You have an excuse. After all, your leg is going to be very uncomfortable for a couple of days. You really should stay off of it. And you've had a shock, too, you know."

"Your arrival last night was a much bigger shock than falling down the stairs, I assure you!"

"You're going to need me to look after you for a couple of days, at least," Justin concluded, disregarding her blunt interruption.

"Somehow I don't see you in the role of nurse or housekeeper!"

"I know exactly how you see me, but that's neither here nor there. The plain fact is you're stuck with me."

"The hell I am! Justin, I have no intention of letting myself be bullied by you!"

"Aren't you the least little bit grateful for my rescue operation?"

"Well, yes, of course I appreciate that, but—" She broke off, suddenly flustered.

"You haven't even said 'thank you,'" he pointed out.

She felt the warmth rise in her cheeks and looked away from him. "I am grateful...very," Cassie said with deep feeling. "For a while there I..." She let the words trail off into silence. How did you tell a man that you had experienced a few doubts about whether or not he was going to play the part of rescuer or murderer? Her imagination had run away with her down in that basement. She acknowledged that. In the light of day, Justin Drake still appeared very formidable but not really murderous. There was quite a difference.

"For a while there you...what, Cassie?"

"Nothing. Thank you for fetching me out of the basement, Justin," she said very meekly, still avoiding his eyes.

He crossed the room with his silent stride and leaned down to capture her chin in his palm. His dark eyes blazed down at her. "For a while there you thought what, Cassie?"

Her temper came to the surface. "For a while there, as I was passing the time just hanging by my fingernails, wondering what was below me in the basement, it did occur to me that if I were out of the way, you would find life greatly simplified," she said boldly.

For an electric few seconds there was absolute silence and then Justin whispered a short, savage oath. "Lady, you're a fool, do you know that? I intend to take all the satisfaction I want from you in a much more interesting manner. If I wanted you conveniently out of the way, believe me, you'd be out of the way by now!''

"Maybe, maybe not," she retorted staunchly, refusing to give in to the chills shooting down her spine. "If you wanted it to look like an accident, you'd have to stage things very carefully, wouldn't you?"

"Lady, nothing that happens between you and me will be by accident!" Justin crouched down beside the sofa and wrapped one strong hand in her tangled hair. He dragged her face close and then his mouth was on hers in a punishing, bruising kiss that was meant to chastize rather than arouse.

Cassie was too weak physically to offer much resistance. He wanted submission in payment for what she had more or less accused him of trying to do and she decided the safest route to freedom was to give him what he demanded. She let herself become pliant and unresisting.

Justin felt the surrender at once but instead of breaking off the kiss he changed the intent of it. His punishing mouth gentled into outright sensuality and the fingers at the back of her head began a persuasive massage that went down to her nape.

Cassie shuddered beneath the heavy, drugging caress, telling herself that she was simply too exhausted from her ordeal to fight. It was so much easier to give in and let him claim his toll. When he demanded admittance to her mouth, she parted her lips obediently, gasping as he invaded her with urgency and command.

Unconsciously her hands came up to brace herself against his broad shoulders and she only vaguely re-

alized that her fingertips were digging into him. It
wasn't until renewed pain shot through her formerly
cramped hands that she halted the delicate assault.

"Cassie?" It was a question and a demand. Justin's
tongue circled the inside of her warm mouth, tasting
and tormenting.

There was a tiny moan and Cassie knew in a dim
way that she had uttered it. Then she felt Justin's big
hand on her shoulder. Slowly he moved his fingers
downward across her sweater until they rested just
above the curve of her breast. Cassie discovered she
was holding her breath. The tension in her was ignit-
ing all of her senses. Oh, God, she should stop him
before he went any further. But how did you halt the
inevitable? And there was such an incredible feeling
of inevitability about Justin Drake. Her mind began
to spin in slow, mesmerising circles. He was hypno-
tizing her!

Justin's hand slid farther and then Cassie caught
her breath as he fitted her breast into the palm of his
hand. She gave a small cry deep in her throat and he
swallowed the sound hungrily. Boldly his hand slid
over her breast and down to the edge of the sweater.
Then he lifted the hem and inserted his fingers to
touch her bare skin.

She heard him groan deep in his chest when his
deliberate movements brought him into contact with
the tiny clasp of her bra. He released it unhesitatingly
and then he was cradling her naked breast.

"Justin!" she gasped painfully, aware of the waves
of excitement and sensual tension racing through her.

"Justin, please stop. Don't do this to me." She hated the pleading sound in her voice but she felt so weak.

"You can't stop me, sweetheart," he rasped gently as he grazed her nipple with his thumb and felt it respond. "I knew that night at Alison's party when I kissed you that it would be like this between us. Tell me you feel it. Tell me you know damn well that there's something unique between you and me. You can't walk away from it without exploring it. I won't let you. I can make you want me. I know that and I'm going to use the information. And there won't be anything you can do to stop me."

He dampened her lips with the tip of his tongue and then began to string slow, languorous kisses down toward her vulnerable throat. This was why women surrendered to Dracula's lovemaking, Cassie thought dazedly. This exhilarated sensation was too beguiling, too full of promise. The senses responded to him so thoroughly that he could not be ignored. She could feel his strength, inhale the masculine scent of his body, see the blackness of his hair, hear the desire in his husky groan and taste his skin when she nuzzled his neck.

She felt the edge of his teeth on her throat at the same instant that she heard the car in the drive.

For a moment Cassie and the man who held her kept themselves very still, as if they could will the vehicle to leave. It took Cassie some time to realize that the car's arrival was the key to her escape. Reality returned and she began to struggle free of both Justin's grasp and the seductive fog in which she had gotten lost.

"Who the hell could that be?" Justin ground out as he got to his feet. "No, you stay where you are. You shouldn't be on that leg yet. I'll see who it is."

The black cat jumped down off his chair and wandered lazily over to look up at Cassie as Justin left the room. The green eyes stared at her.

"Stay off my lap, cat. I don't like you and I don't trust you. Is that clear? I am not a cat lover," Cassie snapped and then felt the wind go briefly out of her as the heavy animal leaped lightly to her lap. He settled down at once and closed his eyes, paws tucked under his chest.

Out in the hall, Cassie heard a man's voice responding to Justin's inquiry and a short time later the two men walked into the library. She looked up to see a pleasant-faced, sandy-haired man with vivid hazel eyes smiling at her.

"Reed Bailey, Miss Bond. My father owns this old heap of a house. I didn't know he'd finally managed to rent it out until yesterday. I just got back from a business trip and he announced he'd leased it for a month to a young woman from San Francisco. I couldn't imagine who'd want to stay in this old pile but I figured I'd better come up and see how you were faring after the storm. Dad's leaving for Hawaii with Mom today so he won't be available to act as landlord, I'm afraid."

"Thank you, Mr. Bailey." Cassie waved him regally to a seat as Justin stood like a dark shadow in the doorway. He looked harder and colder than ever, she realized vaguely before she turned her attention to her guest. "The electricity went out last night, but it was back on this morning."

"Call me Reed," the man said, smiling. He was probably around thirty-five, Cassie guessed, and blessed with that easy, good-natured charm some people seemed to develop in their infancy. Not at all like Justin's dark, dangerous sensuality. Much safer than that. "And I'm not surprised about the electricity. Most of the houses in town lost it, too. Quite a blow. Look, I realize you probably didn't know what you were getting yourself into when you took the lease on this place." He glanced around disparagingly. "It must have been a shock when you walked in the door. I don't want you to feel obligated to stay. I'll be glad to see that your money is refunded. Dad keeps insisting that the place has historical value and that's why he's hanging on to it. Has visions of some historical society buying it one day and giving him a fortune for it. Personally, I don't think there's much hope. Say, are you all right? What happened to your leg?"

"She took a fall on the basement stairs," Justin told him coolly from the doorway.

"Good Lord! Did you fall all the way down them?" Reed looked horrified.

"No," Cassie assured him quickly before Justin could answer again. "I slipped and caught myself. I was hanging on the edge when Justin found me. Never did get to the bottom," she added with a quick smile. "I thought it might be interesting to explore but I guess I'd better wait awhile."

"As I recall there's nothing much down there, any-

way,'' Reed said, glancing curiously at Justin and
then back at Cassie. ''Probably best to stay off those
stairs. I wouldn't want a lawsuit on my hands,'' he
added with a slow grin.

''Believe me, I'll be careful. This really is a fascinating old house, though,'' Cassie went on chattily,
relieved to have someone else around to help mitigate
Justin's presence. ''And I don't think I want my
money back, Reed. As soon as I get one of the bedrooms ready upstairs, I'll be fine.''

''Well, if you're going to stay, I suggest you use
the room at the east end of the house. The bed in
there is reasonably new, I think. The last owner put
it in. It doesn't look like dad bothered to have the
place cleaned,'' he added unhappily as he glanced
around again.

''I told the agent not to worry about that. I'll take
care of it myself. I only need one bedroom and the
kitchen plus this library, I think.''

''Only one bedroom?'' Reed asked the question
very cautiously, not looking at Justin.

''Mr. Drake will be leaving to return to San Francisco very soon,'' she informed Reed smoothly. Justin
said nothing but Cassie could feel his narrowed gaze
on her.

''I see.'' Reed shifted a little awkwardly, as if he
felt the tension in the air between the other two people. ''Well, if you're quite sure you want to stay here,
I can only say thanks. It was the money from the one
month's rental that sent Dad and Mom to Hawaii!
Never seen them so excited.''

"I'm glad." Cassie smiled with genuine pleasure. "Are your parents retired?"

"Yes, Dad was in the lumber business. I've taken over during the past few years and it calls for a fair amount of traveling. Sometimes I think about big-city life but in general I like the coast best, I think."

"It's beautiful in this part of the state," Cassie agreed fervently. "Isolated and wild-feeling. That's one of the reasons I'm here. I needed a quiet place to explore myself."

"Explore yourself?" Reed looked a little blank.

"I'm going to do some painting and writing while I'm here," Cassie explained.

"She's not happy doing what she does best, you see," Justin drawled.

"Don't listen to him," Cassie retorted. "He is a…er, friend of my sister's."

"Not any longer," Justin corrected smoothly.

"No, not any longer," Cassie agreed with a ruthless glance at Justin's implacable face. "Now he's just being difficult to the other half of the family."

"I'm afraid I don't understand," Reed said uneasily, clearly wishing he could escape whatever war he'd accidentally walked into.

"Never mind," Cassie said briskly. "As I said, Justin will be leaving as soon as possible."

"I wouldn't count on Justin doing anything he's told," the black-haired man in the doorway murmured. "However, he will go and start lunch. It's almost noon." With a pointed glance at his watch, Justin turned and disappeared from the doorway.

Reed stared after him, looking perplexed. Then he

smiled in an embarrassed fashion at Cassie. "Sorry if I got in the middle of a fight or something," he mumbled apologetically.

"It's not your fault," Cassie assured him. "He's a difficult man under the best of circumstances."

"You two aren't…that is, are you, well, together?" Reed asked weakly.

"Definitely not!" Cassie's brows came together in a severe frown.

"Oh. I see." Clearly he didn't. "Well, I guess I ought to be on my way. I wouldn't want to ruin lunch for you."

"I apologize for Justin's behavior." Cassie smiled. "As I said, he'll be leaving soon. Forget him."

"Sure. Well, so long. Are you certain you don't need anything? I could probably get one of the women in town to come up and do some cleaning or something."

"No, I'll be fine. I like the atmosphere, you see."

"Atmosphere?"

"Such a pleasant change from the humdrum routine of the stock market." She indicated the pile of books she had unpacked the previous evening. "I'm going to be studying something totally new while I'm here."

With a trace of uncertainty Reed walked over to the stack of books and picked up a few. *"The Right Half of the Brain and How it Affects Creativity; The Zen Approach to Painting; A Yoga Guide to Releasing Creativity; The Natural Writing Method; Poetry from the Heart in Ten Easy Lessons; Exercises to Release Your Inner Creative Forces."* Carefully Reed replaced the books. "Uh, an interesting collection." He appeared more uneasy than ever, Cassie decided wryly. Probably not a creative type.

"It's garbage," Justin said from the doorway where he had reappeared carrying a plate of sandwiches.

"It is not garbage!" Cassie yelped, incensed. "Just because you don't appreciate the new thinking about the secrets of creativity, that's no reason to call it garbage!"

"Here, eat your sandwich." Justin shoved the plate into her hands and then glared at Reed, who got the message immediately.

"I was just on my way. Don't worry, I'll see myself out!" He made his exit hastily. A moment later the front door slammed and a car started up in the drive.

Justin sat down calmly in a chair across from an infuriated Cassie and began to eat the cheese sandwich he had made. The black cat, still on Cassie's lap, finally opened his eyes and examined the sandwich she held. She fed him a piece because she was a little afraid not to, and then she bit into her own half. She refused to speak to Justin.

"Bailey didn't even notice the cat," Justin observed after a few moments.

"Probably thought he belonged to me," Cassie said shortly. "Justin, I meant what I said earlier. I want you to leave."

"Why didn't you ask Bailey to throw me out, then?"

"Because you probably would have made a terrible scene and beaten the poor man to a pulp, that's why!"

"Probably." Justin shrugged, losing interest in the matter. "How's the leg?"

"It hurts."

"Yeah, it will for a day or two, I imagine. After we eat I'll go upstairs and see if that east bedroom is really habitable."

"You needn't bother," she told him stiffly.

"You're hardly in any condition to do it yourself."

He had a point there, Cassie realized unhappily. The leg was still causing her pain and standing on it would be unpleasant, to say the least. "Hand me some of those books. I'll read while you do the housekeeping. Be sure to check for signs of mice or other varmints," she added darkly.

"Hopefully, the cat has been doing his job," Justin said, rising to his feet. He handed her the stack of books, his expression making it plain what he thought of them, and went upstairs to carry out his self-assigned task.

Cassie opened *Poetry from the Heart in Ten Easy Lessons* and stared unseeingly at lesson one. All she could think about was how she was going to get rid of Justin Drake.

As she tried to read during the afternoon, Justin came and went on silent feet, bringing her tea, asking her what she wanted for dinner, telling her he'd gotten the bedroom into some semblance of order. She was half-amazed at his attentiveness and half-frightened by it. It was becoming increasingly obvious that he had no intention of leaving that evening. By the time he brought in a predinner glass of wine and rebuilt the fire against the chill of another rainstorm, Cassie knew she was going to have to make defensive plans for the coming night.

''You're not going to make this easy, are you, Justin?'' She sipped her wine broodingly and watched him work on the fire. He looked right at home illuminated by flames. Justin Drake was living in the wrong century. He belonged to an earlier era. Cassie realized that she had grown less wary of him by daylight. His rescue and care of her had undoubtedly contributed to that relaxation of caution. But now night was coming and already he was appearing far more dangerous to her. He was, indeed, a creature of the night.

''Cassie, be honest. You wouldn't want to be alone tonight in this old house and you know it. You probably wouldn't even be able to get upstairs to the bedroom by yourself.''

''My leg feels much better,'' she contradicted loftily.

''I'm staying, Cassie,'' he said flatly.

''I'm not going to sleep with you, Justin. I swear it! And if you try to force me...''

''Relax. I made up two bedrooms this afternoon,'' he told her coolly.

''You did?'' She hadn't realized that.

''I know when to push and when not to push,'' he assured her sardonically. ''And tonight, after your disaster this morning, is not a time to push. You can lie all by yourself in that huge four-poster bed and wonder what it would be like if I wandered into your room.''

Her head snapped up defensively. ''I can guarantee you that I will not spend my time wondering about that! Furthermore, my leg should be much better by tomorrow morning and I want you gone by noon!''

''We'll talk about tomorrow when it gets here. Ready for dinner?'' He gave her his twisted smile and took her empty wineglass from her hand.

Cassie shuddered as she looked over at the cat. ''What am I going to do, cat?'' she asked when Justin had left the room. ''He scares me in more ways than one.'' But he excited her, too, in a new and unfamiliar way. Cassie remembered his kiss and told herself her own reaction to the man was the most dangerous element in the tangled web he was weaving around her. Why couldn't she hate him the way he deserved to be hated? Why in heaven's name was she so aware of and attracted to Justin Drake?

And although she feared him on some levels and was genuinely wary of him, she was not literally terrified of the man the way she ought to be. That was the hardest thing to understand. She couldn't summon up either genuine terror or genuine hatred. All she got when she tried was a thrilling, inexplicable sense of excitement and intrigue.

Genuine terror struck much later that evening after Cassie was safely asleep alone in the east bedroom.

Five

The flaming coals that were the eyes of the dark creature on the balcony outside her window warned Cassie that she must still be dreaming. No man had eyes that burned with such demonic red fire.

She *had* to be dreaming!

Just as in a terrifying dream, her vocal cords seemed to have lost all power. In those first few paralyzing seconds, Cassie couldn't even summon a scream. In the next few seconds she wondered if it would have done any good.

She had come awake drowsily, some sixth sense making her strangely uneasy. The storm that had begun earlier in the afternoon was now in full action, arcing lightning through the skies and sending the wind to howl around the eaves of the old house.

Her sleepy gaze went automatically to the many-paned bay window as the lightning cracked. And that was when she saw the midnight creature with the fierce, gleaming red eyes. The arms raised, huge wings of arms that reached—

The stunning horror went straight to the heart of all her most primitive fears. Fear of the dark; fear of attack; fear of the supernatural. They were the sources of atavistic dread, terrors that were kept reasonably well suppressed in the modern world. But when they surfaced, a human being might just as well have been living half a million years in the past.

She couldn't even scream.

The lightning cracked again as Cassie lay staring. Rigid with terror, she tried to convince herself she was only dreaming, caught in the grip of a horrifyingly real nightmare.

The darkness of the storm engulfed the window as the lightning faded. The high-ceilinged bedroom was enclosed in pitch blackness. Some vague sense of survival finally jolted through Cassie's stricken nerves. Without any clear idea of what she was doing, knowing only that she needed light to ward off this demon of the dark, she began to inch her way across the bed, struggling to reach the lamp on the nightstand.

Just as her fingers closed, shaking, on the switch of the little lamp, the lightning flashed once more across the sky. And this time nothing at all was on the balcony. The creature with the flaming-red eyes was gone as if it had never existed.

Because it never did exist, her common sense tried to scream. *You were dreaming, Cassie. Dreaming!*

The soft rose-colored lamp came on at her touch, sending a soothing warmth through the old-fashioned room. Breath coming in shallow, shuddering gasps, her palms wet with the evidence of her fear, Cassie rolled to the edge of the great four-poster bed and sat up. She must have been dreaming. It was the only answer.

She did not believe in ghosts and demons and Dracula.

Oh, God, Dracula. The creature at the window resembled nothing so much as some inner conception of Dracula. Those arms lifting high had seemed almost like huge bat wings....

Cassie shook her head, trying to clear it. She did not truly believe in Dracula or anyone remotely like him. But there was a man who had cause to hate her. A man who wanted revenge and who knew she had described him more than once as a vampire. And he had been so willing to let her sleep alone tonight!

Cassie's breath caught in her chest. She had to know. She had to know if Justin Drake would resort to such terrifying methods. A part of her refused to rest until she had learned the truth. Without pausing to think, Cassie got to her feet and hurried, barefoot, to the door.

What would she do if she found him gone from his bedroom? Or if she found him there, but discovered he was wet with rain? She would know he had been outside and there could be only one reason for him to have been outside on a night like this.

She had to know.

Driven by a compulsive desire to learn the truth about Justin, Cassie padded down the hall to the bedroom she knew he was using. The long-sleeved cotton

nightgown billowed around her bare ankles and her
hair was sleep-mussed, but she was totally unaware
of the soft, inviting picture she made.

Her heart still hadn't returned to normal by the time
she reached the closed door of Justin's room. Now
what? Should she knock? Give him time to dry off
and put on a robe if he had, indeed, been outside?
No, she couldn't give him any warning. She would
simply open the door very quietly and see if he was
asleep in the bed. If he was, she would leave as silently as she had arrived and he would never know.

And if he wasn't in bed? Would she dare to confront him if he were standing in the room wearing a
black cape that was dripping wet with rain? What
woman in her right mind dared to challenge Dracula?

Panic seized her as her fingers closed over the brass
doorknob. The fear of what she would discover when
she opened the door was almost as great as the horror
that had shot through her when she had awakened
earlier. But she had to *know!*

The knob turned easily in her hand. Had she been
hoping the door would be locked so that she would
have an excuse to turn away and flee back to her own
room? Now she could only go through with opening
the door and pray that she had been dreaming earlier;
that Justin would be sound asleep in his own bed.

Slowly, slowly, with infinite dread, Cassie pushed
open the door. It gave onto darkness illuminated only
by the erratic stab of lightning outside the window. It
took several seconds before Cassie could make out
the tumbled outline of a sleep-rumpled bed.

It took a few more seconds before her widening

eyes realized the bed was empty. She stood frozen in the doorway.

"Hello, Cassie."

The deep, riveting voice came from near the window. Cassie swung her appalled gaze in that direction and saw him. She didn't know whether to sag with relief or run from a new kind of horror.

Justin wasn't standing in a dripping-wet cape. He was naked from the waist up wearing only the snug black jeans he'd had on earlier. His coal-black hair was rakishly tousled and his eyes gleamed dark, not red.

He turned slowly from the window, trapping her with the sheer force of his will.

"Justin, I...I wanted to see, that is, I had this dream and I thought..." Her tongue felt totally unmanageable. Cassie dimly realized she should get out of the doorway and scurry back to her own room. She'd discovered what she'd set out to find. Justin wasn't dripping wet or wearing a cape. He looked quite dry as far as she could tell. Apparently he'd been trying to sleep, judging from the rumpled bed.

But even as she reassured herself on one matter, another, even more disturbing factor entered the equation. She was standing in Justin's bedroom wearing only a nightgown. He was bound to assume that she was there for one reason and one reason only. Why wasn't she running as fast as she could back to the safety of her own room? Why was she as mesmerized now as she had been a few minutes ago when she had seen the night terror outside her window?

"I wasn't expecting you tonight, Cassie," he said

simply, his voice soft and husky. Slowly he started toward her, the storm behind him creating a seething, incredibly passionate backdrop. Justin moved with that gliding pace that reminded her of a night-prowling cat. And as he came toward her she began to feel as helpless as any small, cornered creature.

"Justin, I…" Her words trailed off as she lifted her wide amber eyes to his face. Even in the shadowy, flickering light, she could read the desire that was flaring to life in him.

"You don't have to say anything, Cassie," he whispered thickly. Justin's hand came up to touch her wildly disarrayed hair and she saw the brief hint of a smile touch his mouth. A smile of satisfaction or affection or anticipation? It was impossible to tell. "You're here. That says it all. I didn't think you would come to me so soon. But I didn't think you could ignore me, either. Any more than I can ignore you."

"Justin, please, listen," she begged, trembling as his fingers stroked sensually through her hair. "I had a dream and I had to know…"

"If it was real? Did you dream about me, Cassie?" he murmured. With tantalizing gentleness he bent his head to feast luxuriously on her mouth. She felt him with every fiber of her being. Her body began to come to life under the slow heat of the kiss. The fire he generated was captivating and her senses responded with a passion she had never known.

Here in the anonymous darkness of his bedroom, with reality distorted by the crashing, pulsating storm, it was so much easier to surrender to the hunger he seemed to inspire in her. In the light of day perhaps she could have resisted, but tonight, her body still weak with the shock of her nightmare and the equally strong feeling of relief in knowing that it wasn't Justin who had terrorized her, Cassie simply wanted to stop fighting him.

There was a strength and solidity in Justin that her body welcomed in the aftermath of the nightmare. It was dangerous to cling to such a man for comfort but she found herself doing exactly that. As his mouth warmed hers, Cassie moaned softly and lifted her arms to circle his neck.

"Cassie, I'm going to make love to you tonight until you can't think of anything else but me," he grated heavily, his mouth only an inch above her parted lips. "Hold on to me, sweet ghost, and let me find out how real you are." His dark eyes burned down into her face.

She could say nothing. Desire was sweeping through her in heavy, drugging waves. He was all she needed right now. Justin was strong and real and safe in a way she couldn't explain. The fact that it hadn't been him outside her window somehow made everything all right. She was safe with him.

Burying her face against the granite of his bare shoulder she wrapped her arms snugly around him and let him support her full weight. His fingers moved invitingly along her body, flowing over her curves until he found the fastening of the cotton gown. A moment later it melted away from her body, sliding into a pool at her feet.

Justin's thumbs rasped thrillingly across her nipples

and she sensed his body hardening. The scent of him filled her nostrils and in that moment she was certain she would never forget it.

"I don't know what made you come to me tonight," he murmured, bending to lift her up into his arms, "and I'm not going to ask. Not now. It's enough that you're here."

She heard the male satisfaction in him, felt it in his sure, commanding hold; but she couldn't seem to fight it. Her head fell back, golden-brown hair cascading over his sinewy arm as their eyes met and held. She could no more have escaped now than she could have flown.

He carried her to the bed and carefully put her down in the middle of the rumpled sheets. The room was chilled and she reached for the quilt to pull it over herself, to shield her from the gleaming gaze that swept her figure.

Justin reached out a hand to stop her. "No, I'll warm you soon enough. Right now I want to look at you. I want to memorize this picture of you waiting for me in my bed."

"Do you really want me, Justin?" she found herself whispering as she recalled his threats of sensual revenge. Cassie longed for some assurance that what he felt went beyond the desire to subdue her in this primitive manner. She was in no position now to demand that assurance. She had abandoned her right to make such demands when she had let him take her into his arms. But she asked the question regardless, desperate for some sign of genuine need on his part.

"I want you, Cassie. I've wanted you since the first

time I kissed you.'' He made the statement almost savagely, as if he weren't particularly proud of the fact. "Tonight I'm going to satisfy that want," he vowed.

She watched, shivering in the cold air of the room, as he unfastened his jeans and stepped out of them with an impatient attitude. The lightning crashed again, illuminating the full length of his hard, lean body, revealing the undeniable evidence of his desire.

Again Cassie reached for the quilt, this time out of some vague notion of protecting herself. He was so strong and hard and dangerous. What had made her so weak a few moments ago? Why hadn't she run while she'd had the chance? Now she was at the mercy of a man she barely knew, a man who had every reason to be enraged because of what she had done to him.

"Do you feel helpless, Cassie?" he drawled softly as he slowly came down beside her on the bed and put out a hand to shape her breast. "Are you a little scared? Frightened of what's happening between us? I can see it in your eyes and in the way your lips are trembling. But you can't stop it now, Cassie. It's gone too far. If you weren't prepared for this, then you should never have come to my room tonight."

Yet again she tried to find the words to explain what had actually driven her to seek him out, but there was no time left to talk. His mouth was back on hers, his tongue moving with imperious strokes to sample what lay behind her lips. The cloud of his crisp chest hair brushed her breasts as he lay sprawled across her body and his muscular thighs pinned her to the bed.

There was no option. She could not escape, and deep in her heart she didn't want to. Cassie's fingers fluttered nervously along the contours of his back and then began to blindly clutch at him as her passion rose with each caress. He wanted her. There was no way he could deny it and he wasn't raping her. She had come to his room uninvited and she hadn't left while there'd been a chance to do so. Because, when all was said and done, she wanted him just as badly as he seemed to want her.

Accepting the inevitable result of their mutual attraction, Cassie gave herself up to the totally unique experience of this man's lovemaking. Never had she felt such uncontrollable, illogical desire. Never had she clung like this to a man. Her nails were gripping his shoulders ruthlessly as he groaned in response, urging her to even more primitive actions.

Her body quivered with the force of the need she felt, a need that was completely new. When his thigh moved to push between hers she surrendered, twining her leg around his and holding him closer than ever.

"You're so soft and so full of fire. Everything I dreamed you'd be," Justin muttered, raining harsh little kisses down her shoulders and over her breasts. She gasped as his teeth lightly closed around one nipple, and when he felt the uncertain anticipation in her body he began to use his tongue to soothe her unspoken fears.

Cassie relaxed again, not really sure why she had momentarily tensed. Was it because a part of her still feared him? Perhaps. In any event this was not the time to analyze her reaction. His mouth was playing wondrous havoc on her skin and she began to arch her body toward him. The soft moans that came from far back in her throat were primitive cries of need and surrender. Justin reacted to them fiercely.

His hands dug into her buttocks, making her gasp again, this time with spiraling desire. Then he trailed his fingers around to the soft, heated place between her legs and Cassie reacted with helpless abandon.

"That's it, honey," he muttered, "give yourself. Let me have all of you. I'm going to take everything, Cassie. Everything." His fingers traced erotic patterns along her inner thighs and back to the heart of her desire. He was sending her beyond the reach of sanity, Cassie thought.

"Justin! Please, Justin!"

"When you're ready, sweetheart. When you're ready."

"Now, Justin. Please *now!*"

"I want to know you need me so much you couldn't survive tonight without having me inside you!" he said, his voice thick with his own desire.

"Oh, Justin, I've never felt like this," she confessed, her head moving restlessly on the pillow as the storm raged inside and outside the bedroom.

"Good. I'm glad!" He sounded almost violently glad. "Keep telling me about it, Cassie. Keep telling me how much you want me!"

"Oh, Justin, I can't stand it. Take me, please take me." She lifted her hips beseechingly and he pressed his hand possessively against her. Then he let her feel the throbbing strength of his manhood, testing himself against her hip.

"You're on fire," he breathed.

"Yes, oh, yes!"

"I want you, Cassie. Feel how much I want you!" Again he tested himself on her soft thigh. She reacted with a soft cry, urging him to her with her hands.

"Open yourself to me, honey," he ordered hoarsely. "Give yourself. I want to know you're completely mine."

Almost out of her head with the force of the raging desire in her veins, Cassie obeyed, parting her legs invitingly, lifting herself against his hand. "Oh, Justin, please make love to me."

Her soft plea destroyed the last barrier. Justin moved at last, settling himself with sudden fierceness between her legs and reaching to grasp her shoulders.

Cassie felt his body move against hers, was achingly aware of the hardness of him as he prepared to invade her, and then, in her urgent need to complete the union, she thrust her fingers through the darkness of his hair.

The heavy, black pelt was damp.

Cassie twisted frantically, unable to understand why that single fact was so significant.

"Lie still, Cassie. Lie still and I'll take you."

"Justin?" The question in her voice was little more than a whisper. What was wrong? Why was it so important that his hair was damp? In the haze of her passion, Cassie could barely think. "Justin, wait, I—"

"Hush, Cassie. It's too late."

His hair was as damp as if he'd just come in out of the rain. Panic began to replace the hunger in her. Panic that combined with her helpless position to leave Cassie feeling utterly at the mercy of the man who was covering her body with his own. His hair was wet from the rain!

Images of the creature of the night who had come to stand on her balcony flashed through her head. "No!" Desperately she pushed at him, denying both the picture in her head and the man who lay on her.

"Cassie, stop it!" Justin bit out. "It's too late!" He closed her mouth with his own, trapping the protests in her throat and simultaneously driving himself into her body.

Cassie went rigid beneath the shock of his possession. Slowly her hands fell away from his hair, seeking his shoulders. She felt taken, possessed, completely captive. Her eyes opened slowly and she found herself looking up into the face of the man who had threatened her with revenge. Neither of them moved. Justin's gaze was flaring with fire.

"You belong to me now, Cassie. You're mine. There's no turning back." Then he slowly bent his head and buried his lips against her throat. Cassie trembled as he used his teeth lightly on her skin. It was erotic and exciting even as it was menacing, and when he began to establish the rhythm of their bodies, Cassie was overwhelmed.

Justin made love to her as if he were intent on possessing her completely, her mind and soul as well as her body. He held her so tightly that she could do nothing but respond, and in truth Cassie didn't want to do anything but respond. Somewhere her conscious mind was aware of the illogical and dangerous step she had just taken by letting her enemy seduce her, but she couldn't fight him.

He claimed her with words that were both frightening and exciting, yet there was an illusion of safety to be found in his strength. When she began to go tense beneath him and cling like a vine, murmuring his name, Justin coaxed her urgently over the edge of desire.

"Yes, Cassie, yes! Let it happen, honey, let yourself go completely. I'll hold you, I'll take care of you. You belong to me, Cassie, *you belong to me!*"

"Justin!" Then she was shuddering in a sudden release that shook her to the core of her being. She felt him arch violently against her, heard him call her name in savage pleasure and triumph and then he was swept over the edge with her.

Together they hung suspended in space, unaware of anything else in the universe except the sensual battle that had just been conducted between them.

Justin felt Cassie's slender body relax weakly alongside his as he slowly and reluctantly separated himself from her. Her eyes were closed and her breasts rose and fell quickly as she recovered her breath. There was a sheen of perspiration between the soft, rounded globes, and another kind of dampness further down. The scent of her was enthralling, deeply feminine and satisfying. He wondered if he'd ever be able to satisfy himself with her fragrance. It seemed impossible.

She had come to him on her own, he thought in

satisfaction. He sprawled on his back, one arm beneath his head, the other holding Cassie. He could scarcely believe it. She had come down the hall in her old-fashioned cotton nightgown, her feet bare and her hair tumbling beguilingly around her shoulders. She had simply opened the door and looked at him. As soon as he realized she was in the room, Justin had known he wasn't going to allow her to leave. Not that night at any rate.

This was how he had visualized her, lying all soft and warm in the aftermath of his lovemaking. He had gotten exactly what he had told himself he would have. There had been both desire and fear in her eyes. She had succumbed completely.

But he wasn't satisfied with the surrender. The realization went through him like an electrical shock, generating a totally unexpected restlessness. He wanted more, Justin acknowledged to himself. He wanted so much more. He wasn't going to be able to walk away from her now. Along with that realization came another. He wasn't going to let her walk away, either. She belonged to him. After tonight he would make certain she couldn't deny that stark fact.

Damn, he thought as his body reached a deliciously drowsy state, it had been unbelievable. Unlike anything he had ever known. He had expected to take pleasure in her but he hadn't expected to lose himself in her. She was going to have to stay with him for the night, that was for sure. He made that decision just as Cassie's lashes flickered and then lifted. Amber eyes looked up at him.

For a long moment there was silence between them

and Justin found himself wondering irritably what she was thinking. Gone was the feminine surrender he had seen earlier in her gaze. Now she watched him with wariness. Justin suddenly realized he preferred the trust and acceptance he'd seen hints of earlier. He wanted much more from this woman than her physical surrender. Suddenly he was no longer interested in revenge, but in something altogether different.

Cassie took a deep breath. "Is it over?"

"That's not the most complimentary thing a woman can say at a time like this," Justin drawled, trailing a fingertip around one nipple as he smiled. "Do you want more so soon? You're a greedy woman, aren't you?"

She moved her head once in a short, negative motion, no hint of humor appearing in her eyes or on her lips. "That's not what I meant. I asked you if it's over. Have you had your revenge? Are you satisfied? Will you leave now?"

He frowned, the lazy satisfaction going out of him. "What the hell are you talking about?"

"I asked you a simple question," she bit back.

"You're the one who came to see me," he growled.

"Yes. But not for this."

"The hell you didn't!" he gritted, anger rising in him. "You know damn good and well you came down the hall to my room for one thing and one thing only! Why are you denying it now? Are you regretting the end result? It's too late for second thoughts, Cassie Bond."

"I know."

"Then why deny that you wanted me?"

"I'm not denying it," she told him with soft candor. "But that wasn't the reason I came to your room."

He swore abruptly, jackknifing to a sitting position, his body humming with a new kind of tension as he surveyed her intent, watchful expression. "Don't play games with me, Cassie. You're not in any position to win."

"No, I'm not, am I?" She gave him a sad, cryptic smile. "That's why I'm asking if the game of revenge is over. I seem to have lost and I simply wondered whether or not you'd be leaving now."

Damn her! She was the one who was playing games! "Cassie, are you thinking that because you gave up and went to bed with me that I'll be satisfied now and take off? Is that it?"

"That's what you wanted, wasn't it?"

"No, it's not what I wanted!" he raged.

"You said that you were going to seduce me," she reminded him calmly. "And you've accomplished your goal."

"You think one night in bed amounts to a whole seduction?" he blazed.

"Well, yes." She looked at him quizzically. "Doesn't it?"

He couldn't believe she was talking like this, as if she honestly thought that his only reason for seducing her was revenge. He was beginning to realize that there was much more to it than that, but he hadn't yet had time to plumb the depths of his feelings. All he

knew was that it infuriated him to hear her talking so
cold-bloodedly.

"Like hell it does. The moment I put my hands on
you tonight I could tell you wanted me. You weren't
here just to buy me off with a night in bed. You were
here because you were attracted to me. And now that
I've made you mine, I'll be the one to decide when
things end. Is that clear?"

"You don't know why I came to your room!" she
shot back. "You know nothing of my real reason for
coming here. You never gave me a chance to explain.
You had to start your grand seduction before I realized..."

"Before you realized what?" he snapped, confusion vying with his fury.

"That your hair was wet," she finished simply, her
eyes lowering.

"My hair was wet!" He stared at her. "Woman,
you're not making any sense." Then he remembered
the way she had gone rigid just before he had taken
her completely. Her hands had been in his hair and
she had gone very still before trying to fight him.
"Why were you suddenly so afraid of me at the last
minute?"

"Because your hair was wet," she repeated dully.
Resentment was building in her. Wasn't it enough
that he had succeeded in his goal of seducing her?
Did he have to continue to play games with her? "I
came down the hall to see if you were in bed or if
you'd just been outside in the rain. I found you standing at the window and you looked quite dry. But I
realize now you had probably just taken off your shirt

and your shoes. You hadn't dried your hair yet, though, Justin. Your hair was still wet from the rain.''

His eyes were narrowed slits of pure, masculine fury. He reached down and caught hold of her wrists in his huge fists and pinned her to the bed. ''Why does it matter whether or not I had just come in from the rain, Cassie?'' he asked quietly, leaning over her with calculated menace. ''What in hell are you getting at?''

''You know what I'm talking about!''

''If you don't spell it out in words of one syllable, I swear I'm going to turn you over my knee!'' he promised tightly.

Her temper rose in her throat, choking back the fear. ''Does it give you great satisfaction to terrorize women who are alone in their beds? Do you get some kind of perverse, kinky pleasure out of acting out the role of Dracula? How do you manage the bit with the red eyes? That's very effective, you know. I was so terrified I couldn't even scream. Did you know that? Do you realize how good an actor you really are? A natural for that particular role. Later when you made love to me, or should I say when you had sex with me, I got very nervous when you started biting my throat. I really wasn't too sure what to expect. Just how kinky are you, Justin?''

She felt his seething anger and she also felt the tight control he was maintaining on it. Never had she been this close to genuine masculine rage. She was learning that it was a terrifying thing. But then, Cassie told herself bitterly, she was learning a lot about terror tonight. The man who was teaching her was awfully

good at his trade. She wasn't sure which version of
him she actually feared the most, the red-eyed demon
at her window or the passionate lover in bed.

"Are you telling me there was someone at your
window tonight? Someone with red eyes? Is that what
you meant when you mumbled something about having had a 'dream'?" Each word was clipped out with
grim care. His eyes were dark and savage.

"Yes! You know damn well it is! Why are you
continuing to play games with me, Justin? You've
gotten what you wanted from me!" she cried.

He stared at her for a moment longer, continuing
to pin her to the bed. Then he rolled off the mattress
and reached down to yank her up beside him. "Come
on. Show me exactly what happened."

"Justin, I'm cold and I'm exhausted. I don't want
to—" She never got a chance to finish the sentence.
He reached down and snatched the cotton nightgown
off the floor, pulling it over her head. Then he
grabbed his jeans and stepped into them. An instant
later he was drawing her after him down the hall to
her bedroom.

When they reached the door it was standing open,
just as Cassie had left it in her nervous flight. The
bedside lamp was still shining, illuminating the tousled bedclothes. Cassie's eyes went nervously to the
window. The storm was beginning to die down, although the wind still howled. With long strides, Justin
went to the bay window and peered out at the balcony.

"Someone was here? Standing on the balcony?"
He opened the window and gazed out into the rain.

Cold wind swept the room and Cassie shivered violently.

"Yes."

"And you thought it was me?"

"You. Or a dream, perhaps. That's why I went down the hall to your room. I had to know."

"And you found me with my hair still wet from the rain," he concluded in a strange voice.

"Yes. But I didn't realize it until…"

"Until it was too late. Until you were in my bed and about to give yourself to me completely."

"Yes." She faced him bravely as he turned to look at her. She could read nothing in those dark eyes, not a thing.

There was a tense silence and then Justin said quietly, "I don't suppose it would do any good for me to tell you that it must have been a dream and that the reason my hair was wet was because I had just taken a bath?"

The really ridiculous part was that she longed to believe him, Cassie realized dazedly. Perhaps it was instinctive for a woman to want to believe the man who had just seduced her. "You're the only one I know who's out for revenge against me," she muttered, turning away to put some distance between them. "It was pretty effective, Justin, if a little juvenile."

"Cassie, it wasn't me on that balcony tonight," he stated flatly. Justin's hand came down on her shoulder, spinning her around to face him. "It was a dream. I don't get my kicks scaring women half out of their wits with Dracula costumes. I may be a lot of things in your eyes but I'm not crazy.''

"I never thought you were. Men who make their living running successful gambling casinos and who set their sights on wealthy young women like my sister aren't crazy. They're considered very, very shrewd and dangerous. Are you going to deny that you're shrewd or dangerous, Justin?'' She lifted her challenging gaze to his implacable face.

"That's a slightly loaded question, isn't it?'' he gritted. ''I might answer it if you'll answer my loaded question. It might have been a nightmare that sent you scurrying down the hall to my bedroom tonight, but you didn't stay for warm milk and cookies, did you? You stayed for another reason. What reason was that, Cassie? Are you going to deny that you wanted me as badly as I wanted you?''

She stared at him with mute fury, refusing to respond. Justin nodded once, as if in grim satisfaction, and then he closed and locked the window that opened onto the balcony.

"Go back to bed, Cassie. I think we both need some sleep. We'll talk this out in the morning.'' He walked past her on his way to the door. At the entrance to the room he halted, one hand on the door frame. ''Whatever else happened tonight, one thing is unchanged. You belong to me now. And I'm not going to let you go until it suits me, Cassie Bond. I meant what I said earlier. I'll be the one to decide when things end.''

Six

Justin stood in the shadows of the third-floor landing and silently watched Cassie as she sat in the tower window one floor below. Her hair was coming loose from its moorings already even though it was only a little after eight in the morning. She was wearing faded jeans, a pair of moccasins and a long-sleeved yellow cotton pullover. Her legs were crossed under her as she reclined on the dusty old Victorian window seat and there was a notepad in her lap.

On the table beside her was *Poetry from the Heart in Ten Easy Lessons.* As Justin watched, her tousled head moved back and forth, the golden-brown hair catching the morning sun. She was examining a paragraph in the book and comparing it with something she had written on the notepad.

The earnest way she was working was somehow reassuring. At least she wasn't packing to leave as

Justin had half expected. Cassie Bond had guts. She wasn't about to let him drive her out of the mansion. The twisted smile flickered about his mouth as he walked slowly down the carved staircase.

Last night had been as thoroughly satisfying as it had been unexpected. But the paradox in going to bed with a woman who satisfied was that a man woke up unsatisfied and hungering for more. It came as no surprise to realize his body was alive with a pleasant anticipation just from watching her. Justin had known from the beginning that one night was not going to be enough with Cassie.

It was infuriating to realize that it hadn't been her own desire for him that had brought her down the hall to his room last night. She had only wanted to see if he was wet from the rain! True, he had been able to capture and hold her with passion once she had walked through the door, but Justin found it disturbing to acknowledge that she hadn't come to him for what he could give her in bed. It would have been much more satisfying to know she had been unable to stay away from him any longer. He wanted her enthralled and enchained in the same bonds of desire that bound him. So ensnared that she could no more resist him than he could resist her.

Aware that his body was beginning to react to the imagery as if he were nineteen instead of a well-worn forty, Justin disgustedly bit back an expletive and started down the stairs.

Cassie's head came up quickly when she realized he was only a few feet away. For a shattering second she was torn between running into his arms and running as far away from him as she could. The dizzying sensation effectively kept her pinned to her seat.

"Good morning, Justin," she managed with a cool, mocking tone. "Exploring the house out of boredom? If you think it's dull after only a couple of days, just imagine how bored you're going to be if you hang around a week."

He watched her broodingly as he walked into the curved tower room that opened onto the staircase. "How bored can I get with you running down the hall to my room every night?"

Cassie flinched, using sheer willpower to recover and hold his gaze. "Don't worry, it won't happen again."

"No?"

"No. I won't let any more nightmares push me into such stupid actions." The self-disdain in her voice was very clear. "Last night I was frightened half out of my wits. When I convinced myself it hadn't been you who had deliberately terrified me I was so relieved I couldn't think straight. The combination of emotions left me quite vulnerable to you, Justin. You knew exactly how to capitalize on my ambivalent state of mind, didn't you? But I won't let myself get into that state again." She was pleased to hear the calm, firm note in her words. Fortunately Justin had no way of knowing how her pulse was racing or how nervous she felt facing him for the first time after the nightmarish evening.

"You won't come running to me for comfort the next time a nightmare strikes?" he asked whimsically as he went to stand in front of the decorative radiator.

The heating system was functioning reasonably well now since Justin had systematically gone around to each radiator and opened the valves. It had crossed Cassie's mind that she ought to thank him for showing her how the radiators worked, but she wasn't in a mood to thank him for anything.

"I would be a fool to go running to you every time I have a nightmare, wouldn't I, Justin?"

"Does that mean you've definitely decided to believe that what you had last night was a bad dream and not a midnight visitor?" He stared out the window, his back to her.

Cassie took a deep breath and admitted the truth. "Yes. I was angry and still frightened and it was, after all, the middle of the night. One can believe almost anything at midnight. When I realized your hair was wet I was convinced it must have been you on the balcony. But this morning I decided that it had been only a dream."

"Why?"

"Why what?" She frowned at his broad back.

"Why did you decide to believe it was only a dream?" he asked patiently.

"Because in spite of knowing how you feel about me, I can't believe that dressing up in Dracula costumes and peering into ladies' windows is quite your style." She sighed.

"You don't see me as a Peeping Dracula?" he demanded with a fleeting touch of humor. He turned to look at her.

"Hardly. I think you're more sophisticated when it comes to revenge than to flit around in a Dracula suit!'' She hesitated and then went on boldly. ''But you've had your revenge now, Justin. Why don't you leave?''

He shrugged. ''I'll leave when I'm ready to leave.''

''It won't do you any good to stay, you know.''

''No?'' He sounded amused. Cassie hated it when he sounded amused.

''No,'' she shot back steadily. ''Last night was a horrible mistake on my part. I won't allow myself to be so weak again.''

''You're sure?''

''I'm sure. I won't be running down the hall to your room again, Justin. Believe me!''

''What if I come down the hall to your room?'' he asked almost idly as he picked up the book she had been studying.

''You won't be allowed in the door!''

''You think you can keep me out?''

''You won't rape me, Justin. That wouldn't give you the satisfaction you want and we both know it. You want to see me weak and pleading for you again and you can't achieve that with rape.''

''You seem to have developed some rather interesting theories on my behavior patterns,'' he growled, picking up the book that had been lying beside her. ''What makes you so certain I won't resort to raping you or trying to terrorize you with a Dracula costume?'' He began flipping through the volume in his hand as if only half-interested in her response.

''I don't know,'' Cassie whispered simply.

He glanced up, eyes narrowed. ''Come on, you must have some reasons?''

She lifted one hand in a small, helpless gesture. "Maybe it's because that private detective I hired didn't turn up anything to indicate that you took pleasure in raping or terrifying women!"

"Gee, thanks for the character reference."

Her brows came together in a quick frown. "But you are capable of other things, aren't you, Justin? You're capable of lying to a naive young woman like Alison!"

"I never lied to Alison," he said quietly.

"You told her you loved her! You implied you wanted to marry her!"

"I did want to marry her. But I never told her I loved her. Ask Alison if you don't believe me. Alison is not quite as naive as you seem to think she is," he added dryly.

"You were systematically seducing her!"

"She loved being systematically seduced." A hint of a genuine grin curved his mouth briefly before disappearing. "Alison got a kick out of being seen with me, Cassie. I was a new toy for her to play with. An interesting male for her to parade before her friends."

"But you planned to marry her, knowing she thought of you only as 'interesting'?" Cassie scoffed.

"I could have handled her. Once married, I could have kept her in line."

"Long enough to run through her money?" Cassie snapped furiously.

"It wasn't her money I wanted, Cassie," Justin said quietly. "I have enough of my own."

"I don't believe you. Men like you never have enough of your own! But let's say for the sake of argument that I did believe you. If you didn't love my sister and it wasn't her money you wanted, then why did you try to marry her?'' she challenged, chin tilted.

"I told you. Alison had something I wanted."

"A beautiful body?'' Why did it hurt to say that? Surely she wasn't jealous of her own sister's attractions.

"No. Oh, she's pretty enough, but there are a lot of beautiful women in the world, Cassie. Many of whom don't demand marriage. No, what Alison had was something I have never had and have always wanted. Alison had status and respectability.''

"Status and respectability!'' Cassie stared at him, her mouth open in astonishment. "You wanted to marry her for status and respectability?''

"Is that so hard to understand?'' He closed the book he had been browsing through and gave her a level look. "You're quite right about my past, you know. I made my money by running a casino. A lot of my acquaintances come from the wrong side of the tracks, to put it mildly. I've dealt with loan sharks, hustlers, gamblers and a lot of other people who don't like the daylight. But I was tired of living my life in the night, Cassie. I wanted out of the world that had spawned me and that had made me wealthy. I had money but I discovered that it wasn't a simple thing to buy respectability. Not the kind I wanted. I finally decided that marrying was the easiest way of gaining admittance to the world that had always been closed to me.''

Cassie watched him warily and discovered that she

was beginning to believe him. It did make a crazy kind of sense. The detective hadn't been able to turn up any evidence that Justin Drake was hurting financially. Cassie had merely assumed he wanted Alison's money, based on the information that Justin did not, at present, have any visible means of support. But there was no reason for him to lie about his real goal, was there?

"What makes you think you would have liked Alison's world?" she finally asked bluntly.

Justin frowned. "Her world has everything I've never had. She's accepted by all the best people. No one speculates about whether or not she's got underworld connections. No one wonders how she got her money or hints that it might have been made in illegal ways. People in her world play tennis and patronize artists and take cruises. They don't even know about the darker side of life. They're completely insulated from it. They live in the sunlight and everyone envies them. People in Alison's world haven't had friends die in their arms from a bullet wound. They don't mingle with people who make a living collecting gambling debts. They don't deal with folks who routinely bribe politicians. Shall I go on? There are all kinds of differences between my world and Alison's."

Cassie eventually found her tongue, seizing on the one item in his list that had truly shocked her. "A friend of yours died in your arms?" she whispered.

Justin's expression became distant and unreadable again. "He was a little late paying off his gambling debts. The guys who went after him only intended to beat him up, of course. No point in killing a client. They never do pay their debts if they're dead. But my friend thought he could shoot his way out of the beating. The enforcers were also carrying guns. They shot him first.''

"Oh, my God!"

"He made it to my place before he died.''

Cassie felt ill. "What did you do? Call the police?''

"The police have their hands full protecting people in Alison's world from people in my world,'' Justin retorted laconically. "They don't worry overmuch when someone in my world gets removed from the scene.''

"But those men who shot your friend," she persisted, "did they get away with it?''

"No.''

"Justin, what happened?''

He closed his eyes for an instant and when he opened them she could see nothing but endless darkness in the depths. "Cassie,'' he said very softly, "that is not something I discuss. It all happened a long time ago and in another world. I shouldn't have mentioned it.''

"You took revenge for your friend, didn't you?'' she whispered.

"Sometimes a man hasn't got options. Sometimes he has to act.''

"Or he can't continue to call himself a man? What a lot of machismo bull,'' she grated. "But you live by that kind of code, don't you? I should be grateful to be alive, shouldn't I, Justin? If I'd known how big you are on revenge I would have thought twice about blackmailing you!"

"Would you have really thought twice?" he asked curiously.

"Definitely!"

"And after thinking twice you would have gone ahead and blackmailed me regardless of the consequences, wouldn't you?" he asked flatly.

She blinked and moved restlessly on the window seat. He was right and they both knew it. "I didn't have much choice, Justin. I had to stop you."

He nodded. "I know. You have your own code, don't you? You feel a strong sense of responsibility toward your sister. Alison told me about it once."

That surprised Cassie. "She did?"

"Mm-hmm. Said that after your parents died the two of you went to live with your aunt and uncle. Alison was only ten at the time but you were almost ready to graduate from high school. You always assumed the whole thing was a lot harder on her than it was on you and you gave her a lot of extra attention."

"My aunt and uncle were kind people but they hadn't any children of their own. They knew nothing about raising a ten-year-old. Alison was so lonely after Mom and Dad were killed in the plane crash. She used to spend hours in her room crying. She was constantly depressed and I worried so about her. People were beginning to talk about such things as children committing suicide and I was frightened she might do something to herself. I spent a lot of time with her, and I guess the habit of taking care of her has stuck."

"She seems quite happy and well adjusted now," Justin observed dryly.

"Yes. She came out of the depression and turned into a happy, normal young woman."

"What happened to you, Cassie?" he asked coolly, sitting down at the opposite end of the window seat and leaning back against the paneled wall.

Cassie hesitated and then said slowly, "I turned out reasonably normal, too. But I never quite fit into the world in which Alison is so at home. I can't tell you how many times I signed up for tennis lessons. Today I still can't serve on a tennis court. The ball goes all over the place. I get seasick on cruise ships. I don't even mingle with the right people. About the only time I go to a real party is when Alison invites me to one of hers," she said wryly. "I just wasn't cut out for Alison's world."

"How did you meet him?" Justin demanded bluntly.

"Who?" But she knew whom he meant.

"Your ex-husband."

"Someone I met in college introduced us."

"What was the attraction between the two of you?"

"He was interested in my money. I was interested in him as a man. Simple." Her voice lowered with remembered bitterness. Why was she telling Justin about this?

"You were in love with him?" he scoffed.

"Yes," she admitted quietly. "He was charming, fun to be with, handsome. When my aunt and uncle met him they hated him on sight and told me he was nothing but an opportunist. I refused to believe them and married him anyway. My aunt and uncle were too kind to withhold my money until I was twenty-five. And I was too blindly in love to stop my husband from squandering my inheritance. He gambled, you see,'' she told him far too politely.

There was a charged silence. "I see," Justin finally said. "No wonder you tend to be a bit prejudiced against my former profession."

They faced each other across the short expanse of the velvet-covered window seat and Cassie knew that he understood her motives perfectly. She also knew he would not allow that understanding to deflect him from the revenge he had promised himself. It was very strange to comprehend another person's motives completely and to have him understand you equally well and then to realize the full implications of that mutual comprehension.

"It would seem," Cassie finally said carefully, "that we are fated to be on opposite sides forever."

"We weren't on opposite sides last night," Justin pointed out evenly.

"Take as much of your revenge from what happened last night as you possibly can, Justin. It won't be allowed to happen again."

He ignored that and reached for the notepad in her lap. "Let me see what you're learning from that silly book."

"It is not a silly book!"

"You can't teach something like poetry in ten easy lessons. Have you ever written any poetry?"

"Well, no," she admitted, struggling to retain possession of the notepad. ''But that doesn't mean I can't.'' She lost her grip on the notepad and watched in dismay as he scanned the few lines she had painstakingly penned.

My heart is a blind and reckless flower,
It opens in warmth and trust in the night
And fades in the cold, bleak truth of dawn's chill hour.

Justin read the words aloud and then lifted his dark gaze to her tense face. ''A bit maudlin, don't you think? Cassie, I don't think you were cut out to be a poet.''

''I'll be the judge of that.''

''I'm involved, too. As long as you're going to write poems about me, I feel I have a right to judge them.''

''It's not about you!''

''The hell it isn't. All that tripe about warmth and trust in the night being killed by truth is straight from our experience together last night and don't try to deny it.'' He tossed the notepad back in her lap. ''Was your heart really involved, Cassie?'' he asked almost hopefully.

''Of course not! What happened last night was pure physical chemistry. I'm thirty years old, Justin. I'm aware such chemistry exists!'' She snatched up the notepad and turned it facedown in her lap, glowering at him.

He smiled at her in an arrogant fashion that made her long to strike his hard face. Her temper was flaring to such an extent that Cassie might have done exactly that if the big ebony cat hadn't wandered up the stairs at that moment and jumped up on the window seat. He sat in front of the window and began to clean his paws.

"How does he get in and out of the house?" Cassie asked with sudden curiosity. She was oddly grateful for the interruption. The confrontation with Justin had left her uneasy and on edge.

"Who knows?" Justin shrugged laconically. "In an old house like this there must be a lot of escape routes for a wily cat like him."

"Well, he must be using some exit because his manners seem decent enough," she muttered, eyeing the cat.

"You mean he's not using the parlor for a sandbox?" Justin drawled. "I noticed that, too. Are you a cat lover?"

"I prefer dogs."

"That's probably why he hangs around you so much. Cats, like humans, are very contrary creatures."

"Does that bit of wisdom apply to you, too?" she challenged.

"I was thinking more in terms of how it applied to you, Cassie. But maybe it does work for me, too. We're alike in some ways, aren't we?"

"Hardly!"

"No? Don't we both want something we can't have? I want to escape from my world and live in the sunlight of respectability. You want to turn your back on something you do very well—making money—to become a poet or a painter. We're both trying to change our lives and stop doing the things we do best.''

She stiffened, not liking the parallel he was drawing. "How long are you going to inflict yourself on me, Justin? How long before you get bored, give up and go home?''

"I don't have a home to go back to," he said simply.

"Everyone has a home!"

"I don't. I left mine when I sold the casino a year ago. I have nothing to go back to.''

"Are you trying to make me feel sorry for you?" she charged tightly.

He smiled. "Could you find it in your heart to feel sorry for the ex-owner of a gambling casino? A man who deliberately tried to marry your sister for ulterior purposes? A man you thought might be capable of running around in a Dracula suit? A man who took advantage of you when you came to his bedroom last night?''

"It doesn't sound likely, does it?" she taunted.

"No. Well, I wouldn't want you feeling sorry for me, anyway," he decided philosophically. "Having your victim feel sorry for you takes some of the edge off revenge," he noted mockingly.

"You're playing with me, aren't you?" she whispered. "You think you can play games with me until you drive me crazy!"

"I'll be satisfied with driving you back into my bed."

"Never!"

"It's amusing when people like you say 'never.' Later on when you have to eat the word I'll take a lot of pleasure in reminding you of the first time you said it." He got to his feet with a sinuous motion and leaned down to run his hand through her listing top-knot. The action succeeded in undoing what was left of the knot and her hair fell lightly around her shoulders. Justin straightened and went on downstairs as Cassie swore violently and frantically tried to readjust her hair.

"Damn him, cat! What am I going to do? If I run he'll come after me and he'll find me. I know he will. He probably has all kinds of sleazy underworld connections who can ferret me out. And he's got all the time in the world to spend trying to exact revenge. And why should I run in the first place? This is my mansion for the next month! I won't let him drive me out of it!"

It would be like walking a tightrope, Cassie realized as she tried without success to go back to the ten easy lessons on poetry writing. It was such a bizarre situation, to be confined in an old mansion with a man she could neither trust nor like. Bizarre and dangerous.

But in some strange way she did trust Justin Drake. She had realized early that morning as she had tossed restlessly on her bed that her nightmare during the night must have been exactly that. A man like Justin would take a far more subtle form of revenge than staging a stupid practical joke. She believed him when he said that he intended to seduce her, not physically harm her. And by five o'clock that morning she had convinced herself that as long as he stuck to that approach she could defend herself.

Never again would she let herself be drawn into a weak and untenable position, as she had last night. From now on, she would deal with her nightmares in her own room and not go looking for additional trouble.

What had happened last night, she assured herself, had been the result of pure sexual attraction and her mentally disoriented and terrified condition. Justin had certainly made no pretense of falling in love and she was old enough to recognize that what she had felt couldn't possibly have been love either.

Love was warm and comforting and tender. Love was something that came into existence between two people who cared for each other, who shared common interests and similar backgrounds. Love was probably going to be just as much out of her reach as it was for Justin, because neither of them fit properly into the worlds they wanted to inhabit.

Cassie looked morosely down at the few lines of poetry she had written. Justin was right. It was maudlin and the meter was probably all wrong. She really knew nothing about poetry and she didn't seem to be learning much from the book. Tomorrow she would try painting.

Cassie was in the kitchen fixing lunch for herself when Justin showed up again. She had hesitated for several thoughtful minutes before convincing herself that making a sandwich for her tormentor was not an act of surrender. After all, he had fixed dinner for her the night before.

"How's the leg?" Justin asked as he took in his good fortune with one encompassing glance and proceeded to pick up his plate.

"It's fine." Cassie followed him into the formal dining room and again they faced each other across the length of the huge old table. "A little stiff but there's not much pain."

"I'll put a new bandage on it after lunch," he announced.

"No you won't."

"Afraid I'll use the rip-and-run method of removing the old bandage?" he asked politely.

"I know damn well you will. I can change the bandage just fine by myself."

"Coward."

"I consider it more a matter of self-preservation."

"If you're interested in that, you'll refrain from exploring the basement."

She looked up, startled. "Why? Because of that one bad step?"

"I had a look at that one bad step while you were listening to your muse," he told her coolly.

"You did? Why?"

"I wanted to see if the rest of the steps were equally rotten."

"And?" she prompted, annoyed with the way he was drawing out the explanation.

"And I found out that the step which gave way under you didn't appear to have collapsed on its own. It had a little help."

"What on earth are you talking about?" she demanded.

"It looks as if sometime in the past someone carefully weakened that step with the judicious use of a saw."

Cassie slowly put down her sandwich, her eyes widening. "Someone sawed through it? Deliberately sabotaged it?"

"Apparently. Probably happened years ago. Maybe some kids did it as an act of vandalism. Who knows? At any rate, I think it would be best if you stayed clear of the basement. There don't appear to be any functioning lights down there, anyhow. You can't see a thing except with a flashlight."

"Did you go down?"

"Not all the way. I just went partially down the steps and shined the light around."

"Was there anything down there?"

"A few old boxes and some storage chests. Not much else from what I could tell."

"Still, it might be fascinating to explore," Cassie mused.

"Haven't you had enough 'atmosphere' for a while? I want you to stay out of the basement, Cassie."

"Justin, I hate to break the news to you," she said very sweetly, "but just because you have intruded into my house and my life, and just because I haven't found a way to kick you out of either yet, does not automatically give you the right to issue orders! This is my place. I paid the rent on it and I can damn well explore where I want!"

"If I have to rescue you again the way I did yesterday, I'm not going to be in a pleasant, chivalrous mood," he warned evenly.

"I'm not overly concerned with your moods!"

"I knew it." He sighed. "First chance you get you're going to go racing down into the basement, aren't you? Just to show me you don't follow my orders."

Cassie lifted her head proudly. "The thought did occur to me, yes."

"That's childish, Cassie."

"I'm aware of that," she said easily, feeling unexpectedly more lighthearted.

"Will you at least promise me that when you make your exploratory trip you'll tell me so I can go with you? I'm the only one in this house with a flashlight, remember? You can't do it without one, Cassie. You wouldn't be able to see a thing."

"I'll think about it," she compromised grandly.

Half an hour later Justin came upon Cassie in the upstairs bath, where she was systematically, painfully, slowly removing the bandage he had applied the previous day to her leg. She had been working on it for several minutes when she felt a tingling at the nape of her neck. Frowning, she glanced up from her awkward position—she had one foot in the sink and one on the floor.

"What are you doing here?" she asked irritably. The bandage removal was not going well.

"I came to offer my services."

"I've told you I don't want your kind of help. If you hadn't put this on with so much tape yesterday I wouldn't be struggling right now. Why did you have to use so many pieces?'' she complained, bending back over her leg to study the wound beneath her rolled-up jeans.

"I wanted a tight, effective seal so the cut wouldn't get dirty."

"Well, it definitely didn't get dirty. Now I'm going to be another hour getting the tape off!"

"Here, I'll do it for you."

"No!" she shrieked, realizing belatedly what he intended. But with one foot in the sink, she was an easy target. Before she could find her balance, Justin had firmly clasped her injured leg just above the calf. With a quick, heartless motion he stripped off the sticky bandage.

Cassie yelled and swung her hand awkwardly against his shoulder, furious with his ruthless treatment. "Damn you, Justin Drake!" He released her and she stared anxiously down at her leg.

"Honey, I've just saved you an hour of torture." He peered at the healing wound. "Looks in pretty good shape. I forgot all about it last night when you came to my room. Did I hurt you?"

"No," she muttered gruffly, gingerly anointing the rapidly healing cut with antiseptic. She didn't want to discuss last night with him.

"Want me to put the antiseptic on?" he asked innocently.

"Get out of here, Justin!" She leaned down and switched on the cold water, caught a double palmful of it and tossed it at his black sweater.

"Hey!" Automatically he jumped back. "You'd

better be careful, lady. You're pushing your luck.''
But his dark eyes were full of rueful laughter.

"You're the one who's taking a risk staying here
with me, Justin,'' she warned him, no laughter at all
in her now.

"What are you going to do to me? Find your own
vampire costume and come visit me in the middle of
the night?'' he taunted softly.

"You'll never see me again in the middle of the
night, Justin,'' she vowed grimly.

But she was wrong. He was the one who came
down the hall to her room that night. Furthermore, he
came at a dead run in response to her own scream.

Terror had once again made an uninvited visit to
Cassie's room.

Seven

It was like waking up in a nest of cobwebs. At first Cassie couldn't understand why she was unable to free herself from the bedclothes. How had the sheets gotten so tangled over her face? She didn't seem to be able to breathe properly. And the room was cold, so cold.

There was a weight across her feet. A weight that shifted. Then a soft hiss brought her fully awake. It must be that damn cat. How had he gotten into her bedroom? She had closed the door when she'd gone to bed. Closed and locked it, in fact.

Struggling awake, Cassie pushed at the tangled sheet that seemed to be smothering her. Her fingers closed around a bunch of satin and lace that was definitely not the plain cotton sheet under which she had been sleeping.

The cat hissed again and Cassie felt a wave of

panic sweep through her. Gasping for air in an attempt to control her nerves, she jerked herself upright in bed. The satin and lace fell aside and she was staring at the open balcony window.

"Oh, my God!" She had made sure the window was closed, too, before getting into bed. The huge cat was sitting on her feet staring fixedly at the window.

There was nothing to be seen on the balcony, but the curtains billowed in the midnight breeze and the chilled air permeated the room. There was no storm tonight but there was just enough moon to make out the old-fashioned wedding dress on her bed.

It was the wedding dress that brought the scream to Cassie's lips.

The cat jumped down from the bed as her startled cry rang through the room. Cassie scrambled wildly for the edge of the bed, her cotton nightshift twisting around her as she swung herself off the mattress and onto her feet. Eyes wide with horror, she stared at the satin folds of the old wedding gown that had been lying across her face.

With the back of her hand pressed against her mouth, Cassie edged backward, blindly seeking the door. Her eyes were fastened on the alien object on her bed. Even as her fingers groped for the doorknob she heard Justin's voice on the other side.

"Cassie? Cassie, open this door or I'll break it down."

Anxious for someone else to witness the scene in her room, Cassie wrenched at the doorknob. He came into the room in a dark rush, taking in the open window, the cat and the wedding gown all in one glance.

"What the hell is going on here? Are you all right?" He reached out to grasp her by the shoulders and haul her into position in front of him. His dark eyes roamed over her. "Cassie, what happened?" His expression was hard and urgent.

"I don't know," she said simply, aware that her voice was trembling as much as the rest of her. "Justin, I don't know. I woke up and the window was open and that…that thing was covering my face. It was hard to breathe."

Justin released her and moved to the balcony window in three quick strides. "Why did you open the window? It's freezing outside!"

"I didn't open it," she retorted, a bit irritated at his assumption. "It was open when I awoke a few minutes ago."

"Damn," he muttered, peering out onto the balcony. A moment later he turned and walked over to the bed to examine the old gown. Cassie managed to flip on a light and together they stood staring down at the billowing folds of satin and lace.

"It's very old," Cassie murmured in awe, reaching down to touch it. "Look how yellowed the fabric is. From the style, I'd say it came from the late eighteen hundreds. And look, it's torn in a few places. Even so, it's beautiful."

Justin wasn't nearly as impressed. He scooped up the offending gown in one large hand and quickly shook it out. There was nothing to see, though. Just an old gown of satin and lace that had somehow found its way to Cassie's bed at midnight.

"Do you suppose the cat dragged it here?" Cassie

knew it wasn't very likely, but she felt rather short of explanations at that particular moment. "Or perhaps it was hanging in one of the closets and he pulled it down."

"And dragged it all the way over to your bed?" Justin scoffed.

"He's a very large cat, Justin."

Automatically they both turned to stare at the ebony cat, who ignored them both in favor of cleaning one paw. He was a large cat.

"He might have been physically capable of dragging the gown over here but it doesn't seem very likely, does it?" Cassie sighed.

"And if we give him credit for the gown, are we also going to decide that he's capable of opening windows?" Justin drawled, tossing the gown onto the foot of the bed.

"Justin, what do you think happened?" Cassie watched uneasily as he prowled the room, opening closets and drawers.

"I don't know, Cassie. I just don't know. Did you see anything at all? Hear anything?"

"Only the cat when he started hissing." She sat down, her knees feeling distinctly wobbly. She was aware of her heart still beating much too fast as the adrenaline of fear continued to surge through her veins. Across the room she caught sight of herself in the mirror and her mouth curled wryly. Somehow she didn't look the way beautiful, distraught heroines ought to look. Her hair was a mess, her nightgown was exceedingly plain and she had a dazed expression.

"I wonder if someone from town is playing practical jokes on the new tenant of the old mansion on the bluff," Justin mused, bracing one large hand against the windowsill as he gazed out into the night.

"I think this is getting a bit beyond the practical joke stage," Cassie muttered. She slanted a speculative glance at Justin's back. He was wearing only his jeans again and the muscular contours of his shoulders and tapering waist were strong and sleek.

And, when all was said and done, he was really the only one around who had any reason to be terrorizing her.

No, Cassie told herself firmly. Hadn't she already decided he wouldn't do that sort of thing? In the warm light of day she had assured herself he would take his revenge in more sophisticated ways. He'd told her he intended seduction and she believed him.

But it wasn't daylight now and it wasn't warm. The chill of midnight still hung in the room even though Justin had closed the window. Right now it was possible to take a far more speculative view of his behavior. This man, after all, had a reason to torment her.

He swung around in that instant and saw the look on her face. "Is your imagination going into overtime again, Cassie?" he asked far too softly.

"It wasn't my imagination that conjured up that dress or that open window," she whispered.

"Want to feel my hair to see if it's wet?" He sounded thoroughly annoyed.

"Wouldn't do much good, would it? It's not raining out tonight."

"You're not a very trusting soul, are you?"

"A woman would be a fool to trust a man who has openly vowed revenge, wouldn't she?" Cassie tried to ask flippantly. She didn't know what to believe. Tension and fear were making it hard to think properly. She had to clasp her hands together in her lap to keep her fingers from shaking.

He stood still, watching her intently. "What if I told you I'm no longer interested in revenge?"

"Then why are you still here?"

"Damn it, Cassie, don't let your imagination run stark, raving crazy!" He swept across the room, yanking her up off the bed to stand in front of him. Black brows came together in a savage glare and his fingers dug mercilessly into her shoulders. "I didn't find that wedding dress and climb over two balconies to get it into your room!"

She caught her breath, frantically controlling her fear as well as her body's reaction to his touch. Dressed in only the cotton shift Cassie felt far too vulnerable. "You explored the basement this morning," she reminded him tightly. "Perhaps you found the gown down there in one of the old chests."

"Shut up!" he ordered thickly, dark eyes gleaming with barely reined in temper.

"And come to think of it, the easiest way to get onto my balcony is to climb over the rail on yours, isn't it?" she continued bravely.

"Cassie, I'm warning you…"

"But I don't understand about the cat. How would you get the cat here? Bring him onto the balcony with you?" She was pushing him, she realized, for reasons that weren't entirely clear. If he was guilty, the last thing she ought to be doing was confronting him with it, not now when she was so helpless physically. And even if he was innocent, he was just as likely to be dangerous. Either way, it was stupid to taunt him with her speculations. But Cassie was too keyed up and too edgy to think clearly.

"Do you really believe all that nonsense?" he grated, giving her a small shake. "Do you, Cassie?"

"I don't know what to believe! I only know you're the one person around who has a reason to torment me!" she snapped, pushing at his chest to free herself. "If you aren't the one who did this tonight then tell me who did!"

"Damn it, Cassie, I didn't do it!"

"Oh, go away, Justin," she groaned, wrenching herself free of his grasp. "Just go away. I can't think right now."

"Are you going to stand there and tell me you want to be alone? Here in this room in the middle of the night with a hundred-year-old wedding dress lying on the foot of the bed and a cat who looks like he belongs to some witch?" Justin taunted her a little savagely, running a hand through his black hair.

"I haven't got much choice, have I? Unless I want to go downstairs to sleep in the library!" He was perfectly right, of course. Cassie knew she wouldn't sleep another wink in this room tonight. The way she felt right now she might never sleep again!

"You can sleep in my room."

She stared at him, open-mouthed. "You must have

a rather low opinion of my intelligence level," she finally said.

"Afraid you won't be able to resist me?" he shot back coolly.

"Not exactly!" she flung at him. "It's just that I'd rather not make it too easy for you to smother me in old clothes! In here, at least, you have to cross a couple of balconies and jimmy a window before you can get to me!"

She'd gone too far. Cassie knew it as soon as the words left her mouth. Hastily she tried to step back out of his reach but there was no chance. In a smooth, gliding motion, Justin was upon her, swinging her up into his arms.

"Justin, no, wait!"

He carried her over to the bed, his mouth set in grim lines. "You want to stay in this room? All right, we'll stay in this room," he growled as he tossed her down onto the bed and stood looming over her. "I'm willing to sleep in here instead of my own room."

"Justin, don't you dare!" she yelped as he snatched one of the quilts off the foot of the bed. Visions of being totally suffocated by the huge, fluffy quilt brought momentary terror into her eyes.

"Don't worry," he snarled, hauling the quilt across the room to the old padded chair. He threw himself down and propped his legs on the threadbare hassock. "If I decide to do you in, I'm much more likely to perform the act with my bare hands around your throat. I'd want you to be looking into my eyes as I did it, you see," he gritted. "Turn off the light, Cassie, and we'll see if either of us can get some sleep."

He leaned back into the deep chair and pulled the quilt over himself. Deliberately he shut his eyes.

Cassie stared at him as she sat bolt upright on the bed. There was no point in running; he was bound to catch her before she got to the door. And he didn't look as if he intended to harm her, she admitted. Justin appeared annoyed but he didn't look murderous. Perhaps her imagination had gotten carried away.

What would be the point in terrorizing her? If he'd actually intended murder, it could have been accomplished by now, couldn't it? She had been at his mercy last night and there had been more than one opportunity during the day to effect a permanent accident.

In the middle of the night it was impossible to sort out the facts. She wasn't going to sleep a wink with Justin stretched out in the chair only a few feet away. But she didn't think he intended any real violence now. Cautiously she reached out to turn off the lamp.

The cat leaped onto the foot of her bed and settled down immediately. Cassie shivered and stared at the closed window. Moonlight cast heavy shadows on the balcony, shadows deep enough to hide a creature of the darkness. In a way, she decided irrationally, it was almost comforting to have another human being in the room. Cassie decided that having Justin nearby was less terrifying than being alone with the damn cat and a hundred-year-old wedding gown.

What had happened to the bride who'd owned the gown?

Perhaps she had run away, Cassie decided grimly. And perhaps that wasn't such a bad idea. She might not be able to escape Justin if he chose to search for her but she could certainly make the hunt difficult!

Cassie bit her lip, her gaze sliding to the still form of the man in the chair. She no longer knew what to think. She needed to put some distance between herself and Justin Drake.

In the morning she would figure out how to escape. There was no sense pretending any longer that she could handle Justin. Whether or not he was behind the bizarre occurrences in her bedroom, he was definitely beyond her ability to control. Her fingers clenched around the sheet.

Coiled in the old, overstuffed chair, Justin lay listening to the stillness from the bed and calculated his next actions. This afternoon Cassie had been reasonably sure of herself; not about to be driven from the house by his presence. She had been wary of him but unwilling to admit defeat.

Now he'd lay odds that she was planning to run in the morning. That didn't fit into his plans at all. She was supposed to turn to him for comfort and security after the harrowing events of the night. Instead she was deeply suspicious.

He didn't want her suspicious and afraid. He wanted her trusting and willing to surrender. How was he going to recover the ground he had lost this evening? Perhaps the time had come to be a little more aggressive. She wasn't exactly letting herself be frightened into his arms! Cassie Bond wasn't turning out to be as easy to handle as he had assumed, Justin decided wryly. He had to find a way to keep her from fleeing in the morning.

There was only one way he could imagine that would have a ghost of a chance. The word *ghost* lingered in his mind and he thought about the wedding gown. He had almost had his own bride until Cassie had interfered. Justin tried to recall how Dracula had seduced and claimed his bride. Then his drifting thoughts envisaged Cassie's delicate white throat and a humorless smile shaped his mouth just before he fell asleep.

Cassie awoke shortly before dawn to the sure and certain knowledge that danger once again stalked her in the east bedroom. Her lashes lifted, blinking rapidly to clear the sleep from her eyes. She had been so certain she wouldn't be able to fall asleep after the evening's traumatic events, yet here she was, vulnerable and disoriented from it.

Desperately she tried to correct both conditions, attempting to sit up and find the lamp beside the bed. What was that weight on her legs? Was the cat still sleeping at the foot of her bed? He was heavy, she remembered, but not that heavy! Then she realized what the source of the weight was.

"Justin!" His name came in a short, gasping breath as her eyes flew open. She was lying beneath the weight of his thighs, her head cradled in the crook of his arm. He was completely naked and his dark eyes gleamed down at her as she laying staring up at him helplessly. "Justin, no!"

His hand on her breast tightened. "You already know I can make you want me," he drawled dangerously. "Don't fight me. You'll only lose in the end."

She shuddered as his fingers moved, capturing the

tender nipple through the light cotton of the shift. "Don't touch me, Justin," she hissed, suddenly more terrified than she had been at midnight when she had awakened to find the wedding gown over her face. "Don't touch me!"

"Lie still, Cassie. There's no need to panic." He leaned down to kiss the curve of her throat. "You were going to run and hide this morning, weren't you? Did you think I wouldn't guess your plans? You've lost your nerve, haven't you? But there's no need to fear me, sweetheart, only yourself. And after I've made love to you a few more times, you'll no longer even fear your own reactions. You'll give yourself completely."

She whimpered frantically as he undid the buttons down the front of the nightgown. One of her arms was trapped beneath his body and when she tried to slap at his hand with her free fingers Justin ignored her efforts. In a moment her breasts were exposed to his eyes and he sighed with building passion.

Slowly, deliberately, Justin began to stroke her, just as if she were a nervous cat he would soothe. Cassie trembled beneath his touch, aware of her body's fierce response even as she tried to control it. What power did this man have over her that he could so easily reduce her to a writhing creature of longing and desire? She had to fight him!

"Are you finally going to resort to rape, Justin?" she tried to taunt. "Have you given up on the seduction? Have you decided you're not going to have any luck with the terror tactics?" When he stiffened and growled something against her skin she realized she had hit a nerve. "Was that the whole point of playing Dracula? Of sneaking into my room last night? Were you trying to terrify me into running to you for protection? It didn't work, did it? So now you're going to try force!"

"Be quiet, Cassie," he rasped, his hand punishing her nipple with a rough action that was somehow as exciting as it was threatening. "Just be quiet and stop fighting me!"

"That's what you want, isn't it? You want me to make it easy for you! Well, I'm not going to make it easy for you, Justin. You're stronger than I am and if you try to force me, I won't be able to stop you, but what satisfaction will it give you? I didn't think you were the kind of man to find pleasure in outright rape. That's for men who doubt their own masculinity, isn't it? For men who have no right to call themselves that. Only a sick mind could take any pleasure in rape." She kept hammering at him with her tongue, the only weapon left to her.

"It won't be rape and you know it. Stop yelling at me, you little firebrand! In a few minutes—"

"In a few minutes I'm going to hate you as I've never hated anyone before in my whole life!"

"I'll see to it that you don't hate me afterward," he promised, bending again to stop her flow of words with a savage kiss.

But Cassie's fear was in full command. She was afraid of Justin Drake, afraid of his power over her and afraid of her reaction to him. Her only defense lay in total resistance and she was intelligent enough to realize it. Instinctively she sensed that if he was reduced to taking her by brute force, he would find the victory an empty one. She had to go on resisting.

So she continued to struggle violently, her head moving restlessly on the pillow as she tried to escape his dominating mouth. Her legs were already sore from her effort to free them from the weight of his body. He was so heavy, so powerful. She felt small and defenseless trying to break his hold.

Steadily he pursued his goal, yanking the cotton gown from her and tossing it into a heap on the floor. Justin chained her with his hands and his mouth and moved to lie along the length of her twisting body. Over and over again he stroked her breasts and the sensitive insides of her thighs. When he did lift his mouth momentarily from hers it was to talk in a low, calming, masterful way that made her struggle even more furiously.

"Cassie, you're fighting the inevitable. You know you want this as much as I do. Remember how it felt before? Remember the passion in you? You were all fire and energy, sweetheart. I could see the desire in your eyes. That's the way you'll feel again if you'll just stop struggling."

"Damn you, Justin!"

"Calm down, Cassie, calm down. Let me love you…"

"You don't love me!" she gasped. "You don't love anyone, remember? You don't believe in love!"

"I believe in passion. And what's more, I can make you believe in it. Be still, Cassie!"

"I told you I won't lie here like a little chicken

ready to have its head cut off!'' Angrily she wrenched
one arm free to claw at his tensed shoulder.

He swore as she raked him. "Cassie, you're only
making this hard on yourself and the end result will
be the same!''

"The end result will be rape and if you think I'll
submit to it willingly, you're out of your head!'' Frantically she threw her hand to the side, scrabbling
wildly on the night table until her fingers closed over
the base of the small glass lamp.

Justin's head snapped up as he realized what she
intended. He went very still and Cassie found herself
tensing in unbearable dread. Neither of them moved.
Justin's eyes glittered down into Cassie's stormy amber gaze and then, very slowly, he lifted a hand to
brush the tousled hair back from her face.

"You'd really do it, wouldn't you?'' he finally
breathed, shaking his head wonderingly. "You'd really use that lamp on my skull.''

Cassie said nothing. Her heart was pounding and
she was breathing in heavy gulps. Every muscle in
her body was still tensed from the battle. She kept
her hand on the base of the night lamp.

Gradually she felt Justin's body relax. He sucked
in a deep breath and rolled off her, onto his side. One
arm shielding his eyes, he lay there for several moments, controlling himself and gathering his strength.
Cassie didn't move. She didn't think she *could* move.

"Obviously, you're not the type to respond to the
aggressive approach,'' Justin finally observed very
dryly, his arm still over his eyes.

"Did you think I was?'' she whispered, edging a

few inches away from his sprawling maleness. Slowly she regained her nerve. She had won. Justin had backed down when he'd realized she had no intention of surrendering.

"It was worth a try." He shrugged.

The casualness of his response incensed her. "Worth a try!" she yelped, catapulting herself to a sitting position to stare down at him with infuriated eyes. "What the hell does that mean?"

"I thought it might be the easiest way of making sure you didn't try to take to your heels this morning," he admitted.

"So it was all just one more calculated act on your part, wasn't it? Another of your incomprehensible little games! Was it supposed to be another element in my punishment?"

"I wasn't trying to punish you, Cassie," he growled harshly. "I was only trying to keep you from running off. The other night you responded to me so passionately. I thought if I could get you to respond that way again, you'd accept the inevitable and stop fighting me."

She was appalled. Holding the sheet to her throat, Cassie swung her legs over the edge of the bed and looked back at him across her shoulder. "I don't understand you, Justin."

"I know you don't."

"What do you want from me? How long is this crazy revenge going to continue?" she demanded dazedly.

He hesitated and then lowered his arm to regard her with dark, steady eyes. "Last night I asked whether you would believe me if I said I was through with all of my plans to teach you a lesson. I'm telling you now, the revenge is finished.''

She blinked owlishly, not trusting him. ''Is that the truth?''

''Yes.''

''Why?'' she asked starkly. ''Give me one good reason why a man like you who believes in things like revenge would suddenly call it off.''

''Because I've decided I want something else.''

''What?''

''You.''

She flinched. ''Justin, I don't understand!''

''I know. You would if you'd just stop fighting me.'' He raised himself cautiously to his elbow, his eyes never leaving her stricken face. ''It's not really all that hard to comprehend, Cassie. I want you and I know that, under the proper circumstances, at any rate, I can make you want me. I'm through with the revenge bit. I just want you. It's very simple, really.''

Carefully she asked, ''You want an affair with me? Not out of revenge but just because you're attracted to me?'' Her eyes revealed her incredulity.

He frowned, folding his arms around his drawn-up knees. ''What's so strange about that?''

''It's a little odd to want a love affair with a woman you hate!''

''I don't hate you, Cassie. I've never hated you. You made me angry and you got in the way of something I thought I wanted, but I never hated you. I just thought I'd teach you a lesson about standing in my way. Unfortunately the lesson doesn't seem to be going quite the way I had planned. I should have known that a woman idiotic enough to blackmail me was a woman who could probably get away with it! A case of fools going where angels fear to tread, I suppose.'' Something close to humor flickered in his eyes for a second. Then he raised one hand to his shoulder.

Compulsively Cassie followed the movement, chewing on her lip as she saw the marks she had left in his skin. ''I should put something on that,'' she suggested tentatively. ''It looks like I drew blood.'' Bandaging his wound would be one method of avoiding the disturbing conversation, she told herself.

''I thought I was the one who was supposed to play the vampire role,'' he drawled softly.

''Don't say that.'' She shuddered, glancing at the wedding gown which still lay in a crumpled heap in the corner. ''It wouldn't be hard to convince myself Dracula was here last night!''

''Looking for his bride?'' Justin murmured.

''It's easy to joke about it now that the sun is coming up,'' Cassie scolded, getting all the way to her feet and scurrying across the room for her old terrycloth robe. ''But at midnight it was not at all humorous.''

''And in the morning light there are still a lot of unanswered questions,'' Justin said coolly as he stood up beside the bed. He saw the way Cassie quickly jerked her gaze away from his body and a tight smile edged his mouth. ''A lot of questions,'' he repeated softly. ''Including the one I just asked you.''

She started firmly toward the bathroom door. ''Justin, I'm not in the market for an affair.''

"Especially with the ex-owner of a gambling casino, hmm? A man you don't trust as far as you can throw him." He followed her, stopping long enough to pick his jeans up off the floor.

"You haven't given me much reason to trust you," she pointed out quietly as she prepared to clean his shoulder. "Will you please put your jeans on?" she added tartly.

"Yes, ma'am." Obediently he stepped into them and then stood docilely as she gently cleaned the wound she had made. "Cassie, I know you don't trust me," he began after a moment, "but if you'd just give me a chance; let me start over— Ouch!"

"What happened to the man of steel who was able to take antiseptic in one fell swoop?" Ruthlessly she applied the rest of the antiseptic.

"I think you're enjoying this," he gritted, glancing at his savaged shoulder.

"The really fun part will be pulling the bandages off very slowly," she agreed, slapping several strips of adhesive over the gauze pad she had placed on the bleeding scratch marks.

"Is that why you're overbandaging my shoulder?" he grunted.

"How did you guess?"

He sighed as she finished. "Cassie, you're avoiding the issue."

"I'm still recovering from the shock of very nearly being raped. It's hard to talk about having an affair with a man who almost raped you!" she flung at him.

"Damn it, Cassie, you know very well I wouldn't have actually raped you! Stop talking like that!"

"How do I know that, Justin? The only thing that seemed to actually stop you was seeing that lamp in my hand!" She whirled and started out of the bathroom, only to have his fingers close forcefully over her shoulder. He hauled her around to face him.

"Cassie, I know you're upset. I know you don't trust me; that you're still half convinced I might have been the person who left that old dress on your bed last night. I know I haven't given you much reason to think I might be interested in anything other than revenge and I know that even if I can get you to trust me, you'll still have the hurdle of my background to overcome. But I'm giving you fair warning that I'm going to have you and that you'll be a willing participant in our affair. We can do this the hard way with me chasing you all over the countryside and haunting you until you surrender or we can do it in a civilized fashion."

"Civilized!" she squeaked.

"Yes, civilized. That means you give me a chance to prove myself. That means you view me with an open mind. All I'm asking for is a chance to show you that I'm not out for revenge. It also means showing a little trust in me."

"You're asking a hell of a lot under the circumstances!" she flared. But she knew she was wavering. If any other man had dared to treat her like this she would have hired a bodyguard or called in the police. Yet she had let Justin get dangerously close, allowed him to make love to her even as she was forced to ask herself whether or not he might be trying to terrorize her. What in the world was the matter with her?

Had she gone crazy? Why was she even listening to him? It was probably only another kind of maneuver. He hadn't achieved his goal by using force so now he was going to attempt a more insidious kind of seduction.

Remember who this is, Cassie told herself. This is the man who was going to marry your sister for his own purposes. And this is the man who comes from the shady underworld of a gambling casino. How can you even consider giving him any kind of chance?

"Cassie, I won't rush you," he vowed. "But I also won't let you go. Accept that much and give me a little time. I know we got off to a bad start...."

"Whose fault was that?" she blazed furiously.

"Yours!" he retorted coolly. "You're the one who tried to blackmail me, remember?"

"Blaming me for what happened is not going to endear you to me," she warned.

He closed his eyes briefly in an obvious effort to regain his temper. "Cassie, please. I give you my word of honor that if you'll give me a chance, I'll back off. I won't push you into an affair."

Maybe it would be safest to agree, Cassie thought, tilting her tousled head to one side as she considered his determined face. She had no way of knowing whether or not he could be trusted, but if he thought she was going to give him a chance, he might lay off the heavy stuff. And if she couldn't get rid of him, the next-safest course of action was to have him biding his time instead of threatening her at every turn.

"No more threats? No more waking up to find myself about to be raped? No more strong-arm tactics?"

A dull red stained his cheekbones but his dark gaze was steady. "I won't rush you, Cassie."

She was buying time, she decided. Time was a very valuable commodity in her present situation. Given enough time, Justin Drake might grow tired of whatever strange game he was playing.

Time was also dangerous, though. Instinct warned Cassie she was already in over her head. This business of giving Justin a chance to prove himself was ludicrous. She should be running as fast as she could, as far as she could, exactly as he had once told her. She ought to be hiring a team of bodyguards, filing a complaint for harassment or taking other measures to protect herself.

Because the real threat in allowing Justin to stay close was that she knew she was falling in love with the man.

She had been slowly realizing it for the past twenty-four hours. It was the only explanation for her own odd behavior.

Only a woman in love would be crazy enough to give a man like Justin Drake a chance to prove himself.

"Your word of honor?" she finally queried faintly.

He nodded, as if he didn't trust himself to speak.

"All right, Justin. For a little while. But it must be understood that I'm the one in command of the situation," she said slowly, thinking it through.

"Cassie…"

Firmly she shook her head, the decision made. "No, don't interrupt. I've decided to give you a chance, but only on my terms. Is that very clear, Justin?''

He regarded her broodingly. "It's clear," he said at last.

Eight

"When can you be packed and ready to leave, Cassie?" Justin sipped his coffee as he waited for Cassie to finish her cereal.

"Leave?" Her head came up quickly. "Leave for where?" She had been moodily reflecting on her rash action earlier that morning, telling herself over and over again that she was being a fool to give a dangerous man like Justin a chance. His question caught her by surprise.

"To go back to San Francisco, of course." He sounded impatient.

"But I'm not going back to San Francisco. Not until the end of the month."

His mouth firmed. "Don't be ridiculous, Cassie. You've had two bad nights in this old place already. God knows whether some idiot from town was playing practical jokes or if it was just a nightmare one night and a cat's trick the next, but it seems to me it would be wisest to leave.''

Cassie looked at him with a stubborn, wary expression. ''You're telling me you think something's going on here?''

''I don't know, Cassie. All I know is that I don't like the bit with the basement stairs or that business of the old dress on your bed. I guess we can write off your night visitation from Dracula as a bad dream, but...''

''You said yourself the stairs had probably been tampered with some time ago as a bit of vandalism. And that cat is awfully large, Justin. He could have dragged that dress around the house easily.'' She shot a grim glance at the huge black cat, who was ignoring them in favor of drinking a bowl of milk. ''Honestly, I don't know why I go on feeding him!''

''Why do you?''

''Probably because I'm afraid he'll retaliate if I don't,'' Cassie admitted with a quick grin. ''Look at him. Would you refuse to feed him?''

''Cassie, we're straying from the subject.''

The grin faded as she realized Justin was deadly serious. ''No. I'm staying, Justin. I wanted a place with atmosphere and I've got exactly what I ordered.''

''Cassie, you're being deliberately stubborn,'' he began heatedly.

''So are you,'' she pointed out coolly.

''What the hell does that mean? I'm only trying to get you out of here for your own good!'' he snapped.

''Justin, as far as I can tell, you're the only one

who has anything to gain by terrorizing me and I would like to make note of the fact that my life was going along quite uneventfully until you showed up on my doorstep! The strange things all started happening after your arrival.''

There was a stark silence from the other end of the long table. Justin contemplated her through narrowed eyes for a long while. ''I get it,'' he finally said in a too even tone. ''This is some kind of test, isn't it? You want to see if the odd incidents go on happening now that you've agreed to give me my chance. That puts me in a no-win situation, doesn't it? If they continue to happen, you'll assume I'm still exacting revenge. If they stop happening, you'll probably assume it's because I've stopped taking revenge. That's hardly fair to me, is it, Cassie?''

''That's not the reason I'm insisting on staying!'' she gritted, but silently she wondered if Justin wasn't right. No, damn it, he was not right. She wasn't testing him, was she? On the other hand, he deserved to be tested! ''I've told you that I rented this place for atmosphere and I intend to take advantage of it. If you don't like the situation, you're free to return to San Francisco. No one's stopping you.''

''You know damn well I'm not going anywhere without you. Cassie, don't make things difficult. I'm a lot bigger and stronger than you are and I can pick you up and carry you out to the car, stuff you in it and drive you home,'' he threatened.

''Ah.'' She nodded wisely. ''I didn't think you meant to stand by your word of honor this morning. You never intended to prove yourself, did you?''

"I don't see how I can possibly prove myself by staying here!" he exploded. "I've already pointed out that it's a no-win situation for me."

"Justin, if you so much as lay a finger on me without my permission, I will consider our deal null and void," she declared in ringing tones.

Across the length of the table they challenged each other, each weighing the other's weapons and willpower. In the end it was Justin who gave in, albeit with bad grace. His mouth in a tight, dangerous line, he silently reached for the coffeepot and filled his cup. Cassie knew she had won. Her mood suddenly lightened considerably.

"Now that's settled, I'm going to get ready to drive into town. I want to check the mail," she announced grandly. Feeling quite pleased with herself, she walked out of the dining room with a regal air. Her sliding topknot did not detract from her air of feminine arrogance at all. Justin watched her leave, dark eyes unreadable and grim.

Twenty minutes later Cassie came lightly down the stairs, dressed in a pair of jeans and a white painter's shirt with a drawstring neck and huge, billowing sleeves. She swung the keys to her Ferrari in one hand. "Want to come into town with me?" She smiled sunnily at a dour Justin, who had been prowling the house.

He nodded brusquely and reached for the keys. "I'll drive."

Cassie hesitated, remembering the Ferrari's pinging. "Uh, maybe we ought to take your car," she

suggested innocently. It would be embarrassing to
have Justin witness her car's unpredictable behavior.

"I'd like to try yours," he countered easily, taking
the keys from her hand. "It will be interesting to see
how it handles compared to mine."

"There won't be much comparison," Cassie muttered darkly. Stoically she led the way out to where
the bright-red Ferrari waited. Resentfully she kicked
a tire before she climbed into the passenger seat. "Behave yourself," she hissed under her breath as Justin
turned the key in the ignition.

The Ferrari, of course, seemed to take great delight
in making her look bad. The pinging began almost at
once and there was a new squeak somewhere in the
vicinity of the left wheel.

"What the hell have you done to this beautiful
car?" Justin demanded, appalled.

"What have I done! You mean what has this stupid
car done to *me!* I'm the innocent party, you know. I
plunk down a fortune in cash for this beast and what
do I get? Nothing but trouble from day one! This car
hates me. Just like everything else I own that costs
more than a buck and a quarter!"

"Okay, take it easy," he soothed, his touch light
on the wheel as he guided the car down the road into
town. "I'll have my mechanic look at it when we get
back to San Francisco."

"It won't do any good," Cassie predicted from experience. But it was odd to hear Justin Drake talking,
even obliquely, about their future together.

A future with Justin? A future with a man who had
owned a gambling casino? Who had once vowed re-

venge against her? How could she even be considering it? Confusion and uncertainty kept her silent during the remainder of the trip. Justin seemed preoccupied with his own thoughts, too, and it wasn't until they went into the post office to collect her general-delivery mail that the silence was broken between them.

"Uh-oh. A mailgram from my broker," Cassie noted with a frown as she shuffled through the small handful of letters. "I wonder what's wrong." Justin waited as she tore open the envelope and scanned the contents of the short message. "Wants me to buy a new high-tech stock that's going public next week." She folded the letter and tapped it idly against her palm as she considered the matter.

"Have you gotten as rich as you apparently are by following your broker's advice? I thought you made your own decisions."

"I do. But occasionally I pick up a couple of hundred shares of whatever she's selling. I owe her a lot and I like her to think I still value her advice."

"What do you mean, you owe her?"

"She was the only stockbroker who would give me the time of day when I first went to her with just five hundred dollars to invest. After my divorce there was almost nothing left. Dane had gambled away everything I'd inherited. When I finally came to my senses and realized the situation was hopeless, I also realized I had very little left to start over with. I sold my car for five hundred dollars and that became my seed money in the market. This broker is the only one who would bother with a new client who had so little to invest."

"So you've stuck with her all these years? You haven't started using one of the discount brokers?"

"Of course not. Like I said, I owe Beth."

"But people who make their own decisions in the stock market and who don't want to pay extra for a broker's advice always use a discount broker. You must have paid a fortune in extra commissions to this Beth over the past few years," Justin protested.

"She's my friend. If she hadn't taken me on after the divorce I might never have gotten into the market."

"You're telling me you've stuck with her and her higher commissions out of a sense of loyalty?" he asked curiously.

Cassie shrugged as they walked out of the post office. "Something like that. I suppose that sounds dumb to you."

He shook his head slowly. "No. I understand completely. In the world I come from you learn to appreciate loyalty and friendship. They're rare commodities." He hesitated and then came to a halt beside the Ferrari. "Cassie, I'd like you to trust me enough to give me your loyalty and friendship," he said very seriously.

She looked up at him in the foggy morning sunlight. "Trust is something that has to be earned, isn't it, Justin?"

His face hardened. "You said you'd give me a chance, Cassie."

"I am," she said uneasily.

"Then come back to San Francisco where I won't have to worry about you," he urged.

"We went through that this morning." She was beginning to get angry. Why was he pushing so hard to get her to return to the city? Before she could go on with her argument, a familiar voice hailed them from the sidewalk.

"Cassie! How are you this morning?" Reed Bailey, her stand-in landlord hurried across from the post office, smiling cheerfully. "How are things going up on the hill? Good morning, Mr. Drake. I see you decided to stay awhile. Thought you were planning on returning to San Francisco?" Reed arched an inquiring brow at Cassie.

"I am planning on returning, just as soon as I can convince Cassie to go with me. Your place on the hill isn't in the best repair, Bailey."

"Now, Justin…" Hastily Cassie interrupted before Justin could launch into a series of complaints. "I knew it was an old house when I rented it and old houses always have a few problems."

"Anything serious?" Reed looked suddenly concerned.

"No, no, nothing at all," she assured him before Justin could interrupt again.

"Good." Reed chuckled. "Thought you might have had a visit from Adeline." His eyes twinkled with laughter.

Instantly Cassie became curious. "Adeline who?"

"Adeline Montgomery. She's our local ghost, you know."

"No, I didn't know." Cassie thought of the wedding gown and shivered. "What happened to her?"

"Adeline was the only daughter of the lumber baron who first built the old mansion. Her parents wanted her to marry a proper sort of man from a good eastern family. But legend has it that Adeline was passionately in love with a disreputable gambler." Reed stopped and grinned. "Sure you want to hear the rest of this?"

"Oh, yes," Cassie assured him eagerly, ignoring Justin, who was standing beside her, his disapproval plain. She waited, fascinated, for the remainder of the story.

"Well, let me see if I can remember how the tale goes," Reed mused. "The way I heard it when I was a kid, Adeline proved so difficult about marrying the right guy, her father locked her in her room until she came to her senses. But with the help of her maid, the girl got a message to the gambler, who sent a reply saying he'd come and get her on the eve of her wedding. Unfortunately for him, Adeline's father intercepted the maid on the return trip."

"Oh, no!"

"'Fraid so. Let's see. The lumber baron hired a couple of roughnecks to teach the gambler a lesson. The roughnecks got a little too rough and 'accidentally' killed him. Adeline discovered what had happened on the night before her wedding. She was so heartbroken she swallowed a whole bottle full of the laudanum her mother kept in the house for medicinal purposes. They found her the next morning lying dead in her wedding dress. Now kids like to pretend that

she comes to haunt her bedroom, waiting for her gambler to come and claim her. The more imaginative
children say that he returns on stormy nights to claim
his bride.''

"Cassie, let's go." Justin put a hand under her arm
and reached down to open the Ferrari door.

"Justin, wait, I want to ask—"

"I said let's go!" There was a steel thread of command in his voice and Cassie found herself obeying,
even though she berated herself for doing so. She was
halfway into the car when Reed leaned down to talk
through the open window.

"Sorry if the story bothered you," he said apologetically. "Everyone around here knows it and no one
takes it seriously, of course. Just a joke."

"Of course," she said distantly as Justin switched
on the ignition. The Ferrari began to ping.

"Say, there was one more thing," Reed said
quickly as he realized that Justin was about to put the
car in gear. "I'm having a party at my place tomorrow evening. I'd like for you to come. You too,
Drake, if you'll still be in the area."

"I don't think we can make it—" Justin began,
only to have his words sliced through very neatly by
Cassie's immediate acceptance of the invitation.

"I'd love to come. What time?"

"Six o'clock. Here are the directions." He scrib-
bled them down on the back of a business card and
handed the pasteboard through the window. "I'll look
forward to seeing you there. Have a nice day." He
stepped back hastily as Justin began to maneuver the
Ferrari out of the parking space.

"You didn't have to be so rude, Justin. Honestly, Reed was only being friendly. Why one earth did you make such a scene?" Cassie scolded, settling into the seat with a disgruntled air.

"I don't like people who tell ghost stories."

"What a ridiculous thing to say! His story certainly explains a few things, though, doesn't it?" she went on wonderingly. "Justin, do you suppose—"

"No, I don't," he cut in ruthlessly. "Adeline didn't leave her wedding dress lying on your face last night, but someone did."

"Or the cat did."

"And the nightmare you had was about a figure that reminded you of Dracula, remember? Not a long-dead gambler."

"But in the dark, with a violent storm all around, they might look a lot alike, don't you think? I always visualize nineteenth-century gamblers as wearing dark, formal clothes, maybe even a cape if the weather was bad."

"It was a dream, Cassie."

"I know, but it's fascinating to think about the implications. Lord! Talk about *atmosphere!*" Cassie stared dreamily out at the passing scenery.

"Hell of a coincidence, if you ask me," Justin muttered.

"What is?"

"The fact that the man in the tale just happened to be a 'disreputable' gambler."

"Don't take it personally," Cassie advised dryly amused at his grim expression.

"I am not a gambler, Cassie. I once owned a gambling establishment but I do not, personally, gamble."

"So?" she demanded aloofly.

"So I just wanted to make that much clear. I'm not going to run off with the new fortune you've made to replace the money your husband gambled away."

"I know you're not," she retorted simply. "After all, since I won't be marrying you there's not much chance of your getting your hands on my money, is there?"

He slid her a cool, speculative glance. "You're really dead set against another marriage?"

"Marriage brought me nothing but trouble. What do I need it for? In my situation it's much safer to stick to affairs." Why were her fingers clenching in her lap? Cassie was furious with herself for the tension that seemed to be seeping into her body as she flippantly talked about never marrying. Surely she couldn't be contemplating something as serious as marriage with this man! An affair was all she wanted or could have from Justin Drake.

"Have you had a lot of them since your divorce?" Justin asked with deceptive mildness.

"Dozens!" What on earth had made her say that? She knew the answer. She was trying to show Justin he was nothing out of the ordinary to her. Merely another man with whom she might share an affair. He must not know she was falling helplessly in love. Her only protection lay in keeping him guessing. A man like Justin Drake would use any weakness he found in her to his own advantage.

"I don't believe you, Cassie," he said gently, the

ghost of a smile flickering about his mouth. It was a real smile, she noted, not his cold, twisted version.

"Believe what you like!"

"I will. Aren't you curious to know exactly what I do believe, though?"

"Not in the least."

"Too bad; I'm going to tell you, regardless. I don't think you've had very many affairs at all since your divorce. Maybe not any."

"You can't be sure of that!" she snapped, annoyed. He was absolutely right and it was infuriating. She had kept men at arm's length since the end of her marriage. Somehow it seemed imperative that Justin not realize he had been the only one who had managed to seduce her since the divorce.

"I'm really very sure of it. Alison and I discussed the matter, you see," he murmured smoothly.

"What!" Astounded, she swung around to confront his profile. "You discussed my love life with Alison? When? How dare you! What did she tell you? It was all lies. She doesn't know anything about my love life!"

"Sure she does. She's your sister. Sisters always keep an eye on each other's love lives. You know that."

"But she wouldn't tell you about it!" Cassie wailed in hopeless protest, very much afraid that Alison would have done just that.

"She did."

"When?"

"The day I told her I was breaking off the relationship with her. Alison and I had quite a long talk."

"Oh, my God!" In sheer disgust, Cassie folded her arms across her breasts and glared out the window.

"I wanted to know exactly what I was up against before I set out after you," Justin explained quietly.

"Shut up. I don't wish to discuss the matter further."

"Cassie, why are you so upset?"

She refused to answer. In fact, she refused to talk at all for the duration of the journey back to the old mansion. When they arrived she jumped out of the car and hurried into the house.

"Cassie!" Justin called after her. "Where the devil do you think you're going?" He walked into the hall and found her frantically collecting paints and a brand-new easel. In one hand she had a copy of *The Zen Approach to Painting.*

"I'm going down to the beach to paint. What does it look like?" she snapped. Head high, she started back out the door, weighted down with all the items she was carrying.

"I'll help you haul all that stuff down to the beach, if that's really what you want to do." Justin sighed, taking the easel from under her arm.

Halfway down the cliff to the beach Cassie turned to look at him. "Actually," she drawled sweetly, "you look rather good that way."

"What way?" He gave her a suspicious glance.

"Packing my stuff around for me." She grinned, her humor restored by the sight of him struggling down the cliff path with her easel.

"Maybe this is why your expensive toys don't respond well to you," he suggested blandly. "You treat them a little rough."

"I suppose you treat your 'toys' a lot better?" she shot back caustically.

"Much better." He gave her a deliberately seductive glance.

"Could have fooled me. Last time I had occasion to notice how you treated your playthings, I had the impression that you could be quite rough with them!"

They both knew she was referring to the violent scene in her bedroom that morning. Justin's eyes hardened but he said nothing.

He sat on a rock beside her while Cassie set up the painting things in accordance with all the instructions. He said nothing as she studiously began to apply the principles in the book, and he watched intently as she chose her first subject.

"That seagull perched on the rock out there in the water should be perfect," Cassie said enthusiastically. "Just see how that scene will capture the essence of timelessness that's so fundamental to the sea."

"Where did you get that phrase?" Justin glanced at her dryly.

"Chapter three of *The Zen Approach to Painting* just happens to be devoted to seascapes," she informed him loftily.

Justin leaned back against the sun-warmed rock and arched one dark brow. "This," he said, "should be interesting."

Half an hour later Cassie put down her brush to examine the watercolor scene she had created with the Zen approach. She frowned critically at the picture of the gull as she wiped her hands on a towel. "What do you think, Justin?"

"The truth?"

"The truth!"

"The gull looks like he's going to be ill at any moment. Maybe he's seasick." Justin peered at the painting with a cryptic gaze. "And I don't believe I've ever seen water quite that color. Maybe that's why the gull looks sick."

Cassie was incensed. "What the hell do you know about painting?"

"I've got a sizable investment in watercolor landscapes of the West Coast," he informed her coolly.

She stared at him. "You do?"

"Uh-huh. I started investing in them a few years ago because I thought that was what people who were respectably upper class did," he admitted. "Somewhere along the line, I got hooked. I'll have to show you my collection when we get back to the city."

"You started collecting because you thought it was the thing to do?" she asked weakly, forgetting all about her own painting. Poor Justin. Apparently he'd spent years trying to buy status and respectability.

"It didn't work. I was just a casino owner with a lot of good art hanging in the casino." He shrugged. "People assumed I'd spent my ill-gotten gains trying to impress everyone. Which was true, in a way. Except that the money was legitimate," he concluded on a harsh note.

Cassie didn't know what to say. She realized she was feeling distinctly compassionate toward him and tried to order herself to stop being so gullible. But women in love tended to be compassionate and gullible and a lot of other things that were distinctly hazardous, she decided with an inward sigh.

"Well, if you're, uh, such an expert, what do you think about my painting?"

"I shall have it framed for my collection," he promised, eyes lighting with laughter.

"But it's lousy art?"

"It's lousy art."

"I might get better," she suggested hopefully.

"You might."

"But you doubt it?"

"I don't think it's meant to be your life's work, honey. I think you're going to have to face the fact that as far as a career goes, you were born to deal in the stock market. Keep painting for a hobby, if you like it, by all means. The poetry writing, too, if you feel you get some satisfaction out of it. But don't try to force yourself into a direction you were never cut out to take in the first place."

"Fine advice from someone who is trying to do exactly the same thing himself!" she couldn't resist tossing back. "That's what you were trying to do by marrying my sister, wasn't it? Force yourself into a respectable life-style?"

"Score another point for you." He picked up the easel. "Ready to go back to the house for lunch? I'm getting hungry."

Cassie wished she'd kept her mouth shut. She hadn't meant to bring up the subject of her sister ever again. What had made her throw it in his face? Suddenly she felt obligated to make something very clear.

"Justin?"

"Hmm?" He was already starting up the cliff path.

She stood at the bottom and called up to him. "Justin, you once said something about me being a substitute for my sister."

He stopped and turned to look at her. She was standing tensely below him, her hands on her hips in defiant challenge, her amber eyes wide. "So I did."

"Well, I'm not!"

"I know," he said quietly. His face was unreadable, as usual.

"I mean, you wouldn't get what you wanted by marrying me. Not in terms of status and respectability. I don't mingle with the kind of crowd you say you want to join, Justin. My friends don't play tennis and they don't go on cruises every year. And the only fancy parties I attend are Alison's. Justin, do you understand what I'm saying?"

He stood silently on the rocks above her, the wind stirring his black hair, his dark eyes deep and thoughtful. "You're telling me that marrying you won't buy me any real status."

"That's right, damn it!"

"But it's kind of a moot point, isn't it? You've already told me you never intend to marry. So the issue of what I would gain or not gain doesn't even arise. We're going to be lovers, not husband and wife." He turned back to his climb.

Behind him Cassie felt a sudden stinging moisture in her eyes that could not be fully explained by the mist from the pounding surf. Angrily she dashed the back of her hand across her eyelashes and picked up the book on Zen painting. Why had she even brought up the subject of marriage? That was the last thing she wanted. It was just that she had to be certain Justin didn't have any plans in that direction, she assured herself as she climbed the cliff behind him.

"I think we're making progress," Justin announced as he waited at the top of the cliff for her to toil the remaining distance to join him.

"What do you mean?"

"You seem to believe that I'm no longer out to marry a rich woman."

"Just one with lots of status, respectability and an entrée into the right crowd," she muttered.

He gave her his aloof, twisted smile and silently led the way back to the house. The black cat was sitting in the hall waiting to greet them when Justin opened the door.

"I suppose he's hungry again," Cassie groaned, grateful for a reason to change the subject. Marriage was suddenly a fearsomely depressing one.

"I think he's got you buffaloed," Justin observed, surveying the cat as it trotted after Cassie en route to the kitchen.

"All the males in my life seem to have me temporarily buffaloed," she retorted under her breath. Fortunately, Justin didn't hear the remark.

The remainder of the afternoon and evening passed in a rather gentle truce. Justin helped with dinner and afterward he poured them some brandy and they sat in front of the hearth, sipping it.

"It really was a lovely old home at one time, wasn't it, Justin?" Cassie glanced upward at the ceiling. Faded paintings of Greek gods and goddesses decorated it.

"Yes," he agreed, sliding a possessive arm around her as she sat beside him on the sofa. "But this would have been lonely country back at the turn of the century. It's hardly a thriving metropolis even today. The crowd that lived around here would have tended to be on the rough side. Lumberjacks and fishermen probably constituted the main social group."

"Maybe that's why the lumber baron and his wife wanted their daughter to marry the wealthy easterner," Cassie decided. "They didn't want Adeline having to live out here. Probably wanted her to have a pleasant, comfortable life back east."

"A respectable life with lots of polish and status," Justin drawled.

Cassie winced. "Yes."

"But people always want what they can't have, don't they?" He sighed. "Adeline wanted her gambler when she could have had wealth and status."

"She was in love!" Instantly Cassie jumped to Adeline's defense.

"She was infatuated. It cost her her life."

"And it also cost the gambler his neck!"

"He was a gambler. He must have known the chance he was taking." Justin lifted one shoulder in a philosophic gesture that consigned the long dead man to his fate.

Cassie shivered. Night had descended once more on the old mansion by the sea and at night it was more difficult to ignore the tale of the two lovers who haunted the old house.

"Justin, what if he really does come on stormy nights to claim Adeline and take her away with him?"

"I can tell you one thing," Justin declared flatly. "If he shows up looking for her tonight in your bedroom, he's going to have me to deal with."

Cassie's fingers slipped precariously on the brandy glass as she raised startled eyes to his implacable face. "Justin, I've told you, we'll do this my way. I am not going to sleep with you tonight! I won't be rushed into an affair. You *promised!*"

"I didn't say he'd find me in your bed. I said he'd find me in your room. I'll sleep in the chair."

"That's ridiculous," she sputtered, very sure that she didn't want Justin that close all night long. It would be far too dangerous.

"As long as you're going to insist on staying in this old place, I'm going to make sure you don't spend any more nights alone. Maybe everything that's happened has a simple, explanation, but I'm not taking any chances. I keep telling you, Cassie. I'm not a gambler."

"Justin, if you so much as try to—"

He leaned down and stopped her protest with a quick, hard kiss. When he raised his head, his eyes were dark and gleaming. "You'll be as safe as you want to be with me tonight, honey."

Cassie weighed the thought of sleeping alone in the room where so many odd things had happened against the recklessness of allowing Justin to stay there with her. She knew she would probably be much safer dealing with Adeline and her gambler, but somehow she found herself surrendering to the mesmerizing insistence in Justin's steady gaze. It would be comforting to have him nearby, she told herself in an attempt to rationalize her lack of further protest.

But she knew it wouldn't really be comforting. It would be disturbing and dangerous. Yet she couldn't seem to fight the dark command in his eyes.

"You give me your word you'll behave yourself?" she demanded.

"If that's really what you want," he agreed cryptically.

"It is!" she retorted staunchly.

"All right. But I reserve the right to revoke my promise if you should change your mind," he teased gently.

"That won't happen."

Nine

He had to get her out of the mansion. Justin shifted restlessly in the depths of the old padded chair and considered his options. Damned if he was going to spend the rest of the month sleeping in this lumpy chair! And damned if he was going to spend the rest of the month sleeping alone.

He turned his head so that he could see Cassie's sleeping form on the bed. In the shadows he could make out the tousled mane of her soft brown hair. She was sleeping in one of the long-sleeved cotton nightgowns she favored. Justin's mouth crooked with wry humor. He knew she found some false sense of security in that cotton gown. Apparently she thought it was as modest as the terry-cloth robe she occasionally wore over it. He hadn't yet told her that when she stood silhouetted in the firelight or in the light from the lamp beside the bed, he could see the gentle curves of her figure very clearly.

Not wanting to alarm her, Justin had waited until she had turned out the light before stepping out of his jeans and sliding into the uncomfortable chair bed. There had been less of an argument than he had expected over the issue of his sleeping in the east bedroom with her. He had a hunch she was a little more nervous about the events that had taken place in this room than she was willing to confide. Well, that was fine with him. It gave him an excuse to be close.

But being close wasn't enough. Justin's brief flicker of humor faded as his body began to ache with a now familiar longing. He had to find a way past the barriers she had erected. He had to get through the curtain of wariness and the sweetly feminine arrogance she used to keep him at bay.

He knew he could have taken her this morning, lamp or no lamp. She was so small and soft. It would have been easy to snap the lamp from her hand, pin her to the bed and overwhelm her body with his own. The thought of being sheathed in her clinging, satiny warmth once again made him even more aware of the ache in his loins. Justin moved, trying to find a more comfortable position in the old chair.

Yes, he could have taken her this morning, but she was absolutely right. There was no satisfaction to be found in breaking her to his will. He wanted her holding him, her legs wrapped around his waist, her nails leaving marks of passion, not resistance, on his back. He wanted her to need him, to cry out his name in the throes of her desire. He wanted her to be able to think only of him.

Justin winced as he considered the trap in which he now found himself. She didn't trust him. How did a man set about overcoming the barrier of distrust? She was quite capable of keeping him dangling just out of reach for an indefinite period. He could easily find himself dancing attendance on her for months. The little witch was more than able to exact her own kind of revenge if he allowed her to do so.

Damn but he wanted her tonight! With a stifled groan, Justin stared upward at the high ceiling. He wanted to be in her body and in her head. Was he going to let her take complete command of the situation as she had told him she intended? It would be courting disaster to do so. Cassie Bond had more than her share of nerve and willpower. She also would not be adverse to making him suffer for his revenge plans if she thought she could get away with it.

The realization amused him in spite of his discomfort. Cassie would run a man ragged if he allowed her to do so. She needed someone as strong as she was. Someone she wouldn't be able to forget when the affair ended and she went on to another man.

The image of Cassie in another man's arms destroyed Justin's amusement. The last thing he wanted to do was think about the end of the affair.

Some affairs went on for years, he reminded himself, although none of his ever had. But Cassie believed in love and that complicated things. What would happen if and when she decided she had found a man who claimed to love her? Justin frowned violently in the darkness. When that time came he would have to do what was best for her.

Which meant he would have to get rid of the other man by whatever means required. After all, Justin reminded himself, as long as she was under his protection, he was obligated to see to it that other men didn't seduce her with lies and false promises of love.

Satisfied with that decision, Justin returned to his own, more immediate problem. How was he going to get past her wary caution? The seduction of Cassie Bond was not going exactly as planned.

Tied in with that problem was the equally difficult one of getting her out of this pile of brick and rotted wood. There had been one inexplicable incident too many as far as he was concerned. Pranksters or wily cats, whatever the explanation, his instincts warned him that it was time to go back to San Francisco.

Cassie could discover her "artistic potential" somewhere else. Little idiot. With a talent for the stock market such as she possessed, what person in his or her right mind would go looking for other talents? From what he had learned from Alison, Cassie could be as rich as she wished.

The problem, of course, was that she didn't appear to want to be rich. Yes, Cassie definitely needed him to guide her. The stumbling block was her distrust of him. She was absolutely right: he hadn't given her a whole lot of reason to trust him.

And right now he wanted her so badly he knew he wasn't going to be able to hang around for months waiting for her to judge him trustworthy. Justin tossed back the quilt and got to his feet. naked in the moonlight he glided across the room to stand beside her bed. She looked soft and invitingly mussed as she lay sleeping. The pale moon revealed the long, thick sweep of lashes that now shielded her amber eyes. Her eyes fascinated him, Justin thought. They had revealed a whole range of emotions in the time he had known her, everything from contempt to flaming passion.

The curve of her hip as she reclined on her side drew his hand with a magic power. He sat down cautiously on the edge of the bed and let his fingers touch the flare of her thigh. If she woke up and found him this close she would panic, he realized grimly. He would have to be very careful. He mustn't ruin everything the way he had this morning when he'd been unable to resist climbing into bed with her and taking her into his arms.

He had been so sure that once she was trapped against his body she would surrender. He had learned differently, Justin reminded himself ruefully. It took more than a surprise attack and sheer brute force to wrest a surrender from Cassie. It had been much simpler that first night when she had arrived at his bedroom door still in shock from her nightmare and seeking reassurance.

His hand began to stroke the curve of her hip, gently, lightly. Slowly the stroking became a little less gentle and a little firmer. Justin tried to restrain himself, knowing he didn't want to awaken her abruptly and have her panic again.

He would just let himself touch her a bit longer and then he would go back to his own hard bed. Unfortunately the chair bed wasn't the only thing that was hard right now. He was a fool to be torturing himself like this. Now he would never get to sleep. He was dooming himself to spend the whole night in a state of unsatisfied desire.

His fingers moved lower on her thigh and against his better judgment he allowed himself to gently squeeze the irresistible shape of her. He was being stupid. He should be getting back to his own bed. If she awoke now he would undo everything he had accomplished this morning with his promises of restraint.

Cassie seemed to be sound asleep. Would she notice if he stretched out beside her? He would give his soul right now for the feel of her hips snuggled against his thighs. What was the soul of an ex-casino owner worth? How much would the devil pay for a man whose past was shrouded in shadows and some violence?

Cassie stirred as he cautiously began to lie down beside her. Hell, he knew he shouldn't have started this refined torture. If she awoke now...

Her eyes flickered open and she turned her head slowly on the pillow, sleepily acknowledging his presence. Justin froze, his hand pausing on her thigh as he waited for the explosion.

"Justin?" Her voice was thick with sleep but not with panic. "Justin, what are you doing?"

He licked his lips, trying to find a way to talk himself out of this mess. "Honey, I only wanted to be close to you for a few minutes. To touch you. I... Cassie," he suddenly heard himself say urgently, "I don't want to sell my soul to the devil tonight. I'd rather give it to you.'' Then, unable to restrain himself, he bent his head to find her sleep-softened mouth.

He had expected resistance, a mad, scratching battle. To Justin's utter astonishment and delight he found a yielding, gentle acceptance that nearly drove him out of his mind.

''Oh, God! Cassie!''

She wasn't going to fight him tonight. Perhaps it was because he had found her barriers lowered in sleep. Or perhaps he had handled it better this time. Whatever the reason, Justin decided he was not about to stop long enough to question his luck. He gathered her close, threading his fingers through her hair as he slid his leg between hers.

He should slow down, he thought, take more time to arouse her. What was wrong with him? He had more expertise and practice than this! Why couldn't he restrain himself long enough to do this right?

''Justin?'' The sound of his name on her lips made him groan. She wasn't trying to stop him, he decided. She was just a little disoriented.

''Cassie, honey, put your arms around me,'' he ordered huskily. ''Just put your arms around me and hold on tight. I need you so badly tonight. I have to take you, sweetheart. I have to make you mine again.

Everything in him was exploding out of control. The urgent pounding in his veins was beyond restraint or logical caution. Cassie was lying half under him and she wasn't fighting him. Those two factors were releasing every wild fantasy he had indulged in since the first time he had seen her and silently vowed to wipe the contempt from her eyes.

His body ached with hard, delicious longing. He could not wait to slake the thirst he felt for her. With a deep groan of desire he caught the hem of the cotton nightgown and pushed it up over her hips to her waist.

This was going all wrong, he tried to tell himself. He should be slowly unbuttoning the nightgown, sliding it seductively away from her breasts. He should be taking the time to arouse the deep sensuality he knew lay within her. Damn it, why couldn't he slow himself down tonight?

Was she going to hate him for his awkwardness and haste? He wanted to impress her with his skill. Damn it, he couldn't stop. He had to take her *now!*

The warmth of her soft thighs was around him as he lowered himself between her legs. He could feel the little daggers of her nails as she gripped his shoulders. Her nipples grazed his chest, hard berries beneath the cotton gown. They sent shuddering ripples of desire through him.

"Cassie, Cassie, I can't wait. I need you!"

She didn't try to reject him. His head spun as he realized she was opening herself completely, letting herself be totally vulnerable. With a husky groan Justin moved against her body, glorying in the feel of her as he buried himself in her. Then she was moaning softly, her legs tightly wrapped around him and Justin gave himself up completely to the passion that flowed between them.

It ended in a searing explosion that enveloped both of them. Justin shouted his satisfaction as he felt Cassie's body arch and tremble beneath him. Then he found his own release, following her into gentle oblivion.

Endless moments later Justin gathered Cassie close, wondering at her unusual silence but too content to question it. In the morning, he promised himself. In the morning they would talk. She had to be made to understand that she belonged to him.

But in the morning Cassie's silence continued. She wasn't sullen or sulky or resentful. She simply seemed to be lost in her own thoughts. Justin awoke to find her already out of bed and in the bath. By the time he climbed out of bed with the intention of joining her, she was getting dressed.

She said good morning as politely as if they had been roommates instead of lovers during the night and then she went downstairs to fix breakfast. By the time he followed her into the kitchen she was feeding the ugly black cat.

"Are you ready to eat, Justin?" With a vaguely polite smile and a glance that somehow missed his gaze, she handed him a glass of juice and carried the tray of breakfast things into the elegant old dining room.

"I suppose we ought to use the morning room for eating breakfast, but this room is so much more impressive, don't you think?"

He sat down at his end of the table, frowning as he tried to figure out how to bring up the subject of last night. Why wasn't she storming at him? Accusing him of having violated the agreement they had made?

Why wasn't she complaining about his selfish love-making, if nothing else? Why was she ignoring the whole thing?

"Cassie," he began firmly.

"I think today I will read the book on how to draw on the creative writing powers of the right side of the brain," she announced, biting into a slice of toast.

Justin's mouth tightened as he eyed her. That had been a deliberate evasion, he felt certain. She looked so innocent sitting there at the far end of the table with her topknot of hair already sliding precariously to one side and several tendrils drifting around her shoulders. The brightly striped T-shirt and the snug, faded jeans she wore made her look as if she were designed to spend her life playing on the beach.

"Cassie," he tried again, making his voice very deliberate, "I think we should talk."

"Umm. Later, though, Justin. I want to get started reading that book so I can try my hand at the actual writing process this afternoon."

"Damn it, Cassie, you're not going to learn how to write by reading a book! Those kinds of books are ripoffs!"

"You would know, of course?" she said sweetly.

"It's obvious!" Talk about stupidity! Now he was losing his temper with her and that was the last thing he wanted to do.

"Oh. Well, if you don't mind, I think I will decide that for myself. It's your turn to wash the breakfast dishes," she concluded, rising briskly from the table and slipping out of the room.

Justin glared at the dishes she had left for him to

do. For the past couple of mornings they had been washing up together. What was this business about it being his turn?

Somehow she managed to keep him off-balance for the rest of the day. Justin couldn't quite figure out what was happening but he was beginning to suspect he was being manipulated.

At least that was what he thought one moment. The next he wondered if he had simply missed something crucial somewhere along the line. When he cornered her in the library where she was intently reading her book on creative writing he thought he had her finally.

"Cassie," he announced, blocking the door with his body. "I want to talk to you about last night."

"That reminds me," she countered brightly, lifting her head, "don't forget we have that party to go to tonight."

"I fail to see how tonight has anything to do with last night!"

"Night comes around with great regularity, Justin. Don't you know that?" She closed the book. "Let's go for a walk on the beach."

He hesitated, wondering if she was evading him again. Then he nodded. After all, if she took a walk with him, he stood a pretty good chance of getting her to discuss the issue that lay between them.

But somehow it just didn't prove easy to do. In the first place there was a brisk breeze coming in off the ocean. Also the surf was high. The combination made it difficult to carry on a low, intense discussion. Every time he tried, Cassie left his side to examine shells or crabs or some other form of sea life. It took Justin about twenty minutes to realize she had no intention of talking.

Then he began wondering why.

What was going on in that eccentric head of hers? What was she plotting or planning? What did she really think about last night?

She had never had much reason to trust him, he reflected. What if she had now decided that it would be safest to simply ignore him until she could figure out a way to escape? Moodily Justin became much quieter himself. He stopped trying to force the conversation as he started wondering what Cassie was really thinking.

She must be plotting to escape him. That had to be it. She didn't trust him and she knew she couldn't fight him physically, so she was going to play it light and cool until she could figure out how to get away from him.

Didn't she realize that, no matter where she went, he would follow her and drag her home? She belonged to him now.

Later in the day, as she busied herself at the old-fashioned writing desk in the library, he thought about bringing up his arguments for leaving the old mansion and going back to San Francisco. But something told him she would ignore those comments just as thoroughly as she had ignored his attempts to discuss their relationship.

He'd just keep an eye on her for a while, he vowed as he selected an old, worn volume of history from one of the bookcases. He'd wait to see if she was planning to run. Then, when she tried it, he would put a fast, firm halt to the attempt. when she finally realized there was no point in trying to evade him, he would sit her down and have a long, hard talk.

Satisfied that he was handling a difficult situation in the best-possible manner under the circumstances, Justin spent the rest of the afternoon trying to concentrate on his book. Every time Cassie left the library to fix a pot of tea or take a short stretch, he listened intently to be certain she wasn't going upstairs to get the keys to the Ferrari.

She'd probably make her try at night, he decided. He would have to be especially alert in the evenings. Justin's mouth curled wryly. He wasn't going to get much sleep until Cassie had accepted the situation.

"I thought we should get there around seven," Cassie said over dinner.

"Get where?" He looked at her blankly, his thoughts on other matters.

"Reed's party!"

"Oh. All right. Seven." He went back to his food, not particularly interested in Reed Bailey or his party.

When they found Bailey's house perched along the cliffs on the other end of town from the old mansion, Justin decided he never would be able to work up much interest in Bailey's party. He just didn't like Reed Bailey or the way the man hung around Cassie.

If he learned about Cassie's Midas touch, Bailey would probably really make a play for her, Justin decided. There was something a little too open and friendly and pleasant about Reed Bailey. Justin didn't like him a bit and he especially didn't like the way the man was monopolizing Cassie.

What the hell was the matter with Cassie, anyway? She had hardly spoken to him all day and now here she was, chatty as hell with Bailey. Justin helped himself to another glass of wine and wondered how long he'd let Cassie stay at the party before he took her back to the mansion.

The spacious home was crowded tonight. Just about everyone in town must have been invited. But then, that would be the logical way to give a party in a small village. Anyone left out would feel mortally offended. He was considering that when he looked up to find a tall, redheaded woman bearing down on him. She reminded him a little of Alison, although Alison was blond. There was that same look of serene sophistication about her. She was also quite beautiful.

"Hi, I'm Evelyn Anderson. I understand you're another temporary visitor in the area. Which cottage are you renting? I have the one down the road about half a mile."

"I'm staying at the old mansion on the hill," Justin admitted, trying to see where Cassie had disappeared to. She had been standing near the sliding-glass doors a few minutes ago, talking to Bailey.

"That old place? How fascinating! I hear they're trying to get it classified as an historical landmark. What are you doing in this godforsaken town? I'm here because I thought it would be a good place to get myself together after my last divorce. So depressing, you know. Richard was an absolute bastard about the settlement. Not nearly as generous as Henry was. The next time I marry I'm going to have a written contract. The only way to go these days, don't you think?''

''Er, excuse me,'' Justin murmured, edging aside, ''I seem to have lost track of someone.''

''Oh, really, who?''

''The woman I'm trying to seduce.''

Evelyn Anderson smiled charmingly. ''Look no further. My divorce will be final in a few weeks.'' She linked her arm through Justin's and leaned close. ''And I have been so very bored down here at the beach. I was thinking of returning to L.A. in the morning. If you're equally bored, however, perhaps we could arrange to amuse each other.''

''Excuse me,'' Justin repeated evenly, ''but I'm not exactly bored. I have never been less bored in my life. Would you please let go of my arm?''

''But if I'm not boring you, why do you want me to let go?'' She smiled sunnily.

''You misunderstand. It's the lady I'm looking for who is responsible for keeping me from boredom. Now, if you don't mind, I have to leave.''

Evelyn Anderson pouted prettily. ''You know, you remind me of someone.''

''I know. Count Dracula. It happens a lot. Excuse me.'' Justin firmly disengaged himself and set off through the crowd. He was taller than most of the people around him and he ought to have been able to spot Cassie's fraying hairstyle easily. But he didn't see her anywhere.

If Reed Bailey had taken her out onto the deck for a breath of fresh air and a quick grope, he was going to be very sorry. Justin decided he'd flatten the other man if he found him alone with Cassie.

But they weren't together out on the deck. Justin moved to the edge and looked down over the railing. There was another storm coming in. The wind was high and the cloud cover was shielding the moon. It was difficult to see anything on the cliff path below the deck. Damn it, where the hell was Cassie?

Maybe she'd been foolish enough to actually let Bailey take her for a walk on the path below. For a bright woman, she could be awfully dumb. Didn't she know he'd never tolerate her playing games like that with other men? Had she done it to taunt him? Justin wondered as he found the stairs that led down the deck to the path. Perhaps she was trying to make him jealous. Would Cassie deliberately do that?

No, that didn't make any sense. Cassie was hardly likely to play that sort of game when she was in the middle of planning an escape from him! Little fool, he thought as he started to walk along the path, peering into the shadows around him. Where had she gone?

"Cassie!" He called her name, but the strengthening wind whipped it from his mouth and blew it away. "Cassie!"

He quickened his pace, grateful for his good night vision. Where the devil was she? How far would she walk with Bailey? Damn, it was cold out here and she hadn't been wearing her jacket over the jeans she had decided to wear to the casual party. She had been the only woman in the room in jeans and somehow all the others had seemed overdressed.

"Cassie! Answer me!" Only the pounding surf below the cliffs responded.

Then he heard it, the faintest of pleading calls. It was a barely audible sound amid the wind and the waves but Justin had been listening for anything at all out of the ordinary.

"Help! Over here!"

Breaking into a run, Justin homed in on the faint cry, following it to the edge of the cliff before he realized it was coming from the rocks below.

"Oh, my God! Cassie!" The words were a tight exclamation from between his teeth as he looked down to see her sprawled on a rock several feet below the top of the cliffs.

She looked up and saw him just as the clouds parted long enough to let the moon illuminate the scene. Her face was tense with fear and in that moment Justin knew a strange new fear of his own.

Slowly, shakily, she got to her feet, her eyes never leaving his face. It was clear she was favoring her right ankle. She was lucky if a sprained ankle was all that was wrong with her. It had been a wicked, if blessedly short, fall. The rocks made a very unforgiving surface. A couple of feet farther along in either direction and she would have missed the rock she had landed on and gone all the way down to the beach. She could easily have been knocked unconscious by the force of the impact and then drowned in the rising tide. Justin realized he was almost shaking in reaction to his own wild imaginings. Cassie might have been killed!

He crouched at the top of the cliff. "Cassie, are you all right?"

"I'm alive, if that's what you mean," she said so quietly he could barely hear her.

"Look, I'm going to lower my belt." He unclasped the wide leather belt from his waist and went down flat on his stomach. "Wrap it around your wrist and I'll pull you up. Come on, honey, don't be afraid. It's only a few feet. You'll be okay." Deliberately he tried to soothe her fears as he dangled the belt over the rocks. She could just barely reach it.

"Will I be okay, Justin?" Her voice was softer than ever as she stood with her face turned up to his. In the moonlight he could read the stark fear still etched in her expression.

"Cassie, what's wrong? Take hold of the belt! You're cold and wet and after a fall like that you'll be in shock."

"I didn't fall, Justin. I was pushed," she said simply. Her fingertips brushed the end of the belt but she made no move to grab hold of it.

And suddenly he understood. She had been pushed over the edge of the cliff and the most likely candidate for the role of assailant was himself.

As far as Cassie was concerned, he, Justin, was the only person around who had a reason to shove her over a cliff. And if, after she grabbed the belt, he were to swing it a couple of feet to the side and release his end, she would plummet down to the bottom of the cliff.

He was telling her to trust him with her life and he'd never given her any reason to trust him at all.

Justin felt rage well up inside. Who the hell was Cassie Bond to doubt him? She belonged to him!

"Goddamn it, Cassie!" he roared above the sound of the crashing surf. "Take hold of that belt. If I'd wanted to kill you, I wouldn't have botched the job like this. I'm not the one who pushed you over this damn cliff! You belong to me and I take care of what belongs to me. Grab the belt this minute or I'll beat the living daylights out of you when I get you off that rock! Do you hear me, woman?"

There was an electric moment on the rock below as Cassie continued to stare up at Justin's furious face. In that charged instant she realized a critical truth.

Love involved trust.

She reached for the belt. "I hear you, Justin," she said very meekly.

Ten

The black Ferrari knifed through the darkness, racing toward the mansion on the hill outside of town. In the passenger seat Cassie sat wrapped in her jacket, shivering as the warmth of the heater began to permeate the car.

"You're lucky," she mumbled. "Your heater works."

Justin didn't appear to hear her. His profile seemed set in granite as he drove with deadly attention. "We're going to go back to that mausoleum, get you into a warm bath, have a hot drink and then we're going to pack and leave."

"Tonight?" she asked in surprise. Everything seemed all right now that she was safe with Justin. She huddled deeper into her jacket. "I'm so tired, Justin. Couldn't we spend the night there and leave in the morning?"

"Not a chance. We're going to call the cops from a roadside motel and tell them everything that's happened," he snapped. "Didn't you get a look at whoever pushed you? Didn't you see anything?"

"No." Cassie shivered with remembered fear. "It all happened so quickly. One minute I was standing on the cliff path admiring the view and the next thing I knew something or someone shoved me in the middle of the back." The horror of that moment would stay with her for a long while.

"You were so damn lucky that outcropping of rock was between you and the beach."

Cassie smiled wanly. "Yes."

"Damn it, Cassie, what were you doing on that path anyhow?" Justin continued angrily. He had been angry from the moment he had rescued her.

"I've told you. Reed suggested I take a look at the view from out there."

"And you fell for that old line?"

"He didn't come with me! I went alone!" Cassie realized she was getting a little angry herself.

"Sure you did!" Justin scoffed as he pulled the Ferrari into the driveway of the old mansion and parked it next to the red car.

"It's the truth, Justin!"

"Come on, get out of the car. I want you in a warm bath as soon as possible." He yanked open the door and hauled her out, lifting her into his arms.

"Justin, stop manhandling me. You've been pushing me around since you pulled me up that cliff. You didn't even let me go inside and say good-bye to our host!" Justin had rushed her straight from the cliff path to the warmth of the Ferrari. No one at the party even knew they had left.

"I'll manhandle you all I want," he grated, cradling her with one arm as he fumbled with the key to the porte cochere door. "It's my right."

"Your right!" she blazed, turning an infuriated gaze up at him. "What the hell do you mean, your 'right'?! Just because I love you, Justin Drake, that does not mean you have any 'rights' over me!"

The door swung open on her last words and Justin halted on the threshold as Reed Bailey's voice came out of the darkness.

"How touching," Bailey remarked, walking forward so that they could see the gun in his hand. "And how stupid. So you made it back up the cliff, hmm, Cassie? A pity you didn't stay a little longer at the party, Drake. It was a mistake to come back here so soon. A grave mistake."

Justin swore softly and slowly began to lower Cassie to her feet. She could feel the tension vibrating through him. His eyes never left Bailey's face.

"No, don't put her down, Drake. I prefer you to have your hands fully occupied for the present. It will keep you from trying any foolish tricks. Bring her along. I haven't got much time. My business partner will be here at any moment. I do not want him to think anything's out of the ordinary. He gets nervous easily. Move!"

Justin hesitated and then obeyed. Still cradling Cassie in his arms, he allowed himself to be herded down the hall.

Cassie bit her lip anxiously as she realized their destination.

"Stand back," Reed drawled with mocking politeness. "I'll get the door for you." He yanked open the door above the basement staircase. "Down there. And I would advise you to stay very quiet until after my visitor has left. As I said, he gets nervous. If he thought there were any witnesses around he'd want to make sure they were dead before he left the house."

There was the sound of a car's engine above the rising howl of the wind. The storm was getting thicker around the old house. Cassie felt her heart beating far too rapidly as Justin stepped down on the first stair. The door swung shut with a sound of great finality and they were plunged into darkness. There was no question but that it was locked behind them.

"I'm going to set you down on the step, Cassie. Be careful. Will your ankle hold?"

"Yes. It hurts but it's not sprained all that badly." He eased her down until she found her footing. "I can't see a thing. Where's your famous flashlight?"

"Where it won't do us any good. Upstairs in your bedroom," he grunted. Then he took her hand and started slowly down the stairs. "Watch out. Remember the one you nearly did yourself in on before."

Very cautiously he guided her down the steps until they were standing on the clammy brick floor at the bottom. It was pitch black in the basement, but the chilled, damp feel of the place didn't need to be seen in order to be felt.

Clinging to Justin's arm, Cassie took comfort in his

warmth. "I suppose it must have been Reed who assisted me over that cliff." She sighed.

Justin's arm tightened around her shoulder. "I'll kill him."

Cassie shivered with something other than the chill of the basement. Justin's words had the simple, flat quality of an immutable law of nature. "If we get out of this," she said very deliberately, "we'll turn him over to the cops."

"They can have the body." She could almost see his careless shrug.

"Justin," she pleaded, "I know you're big on things like revenge and teaching people not to get in your way, but I will not have you committing murder on my behalf!" Cassie felt him moving toward the far wall. There was a preoccupied air about him that said he wasn't really listening to her. "Justin?"

"Here. I thought I remembered that one of the old chests was against this wall. Sit down, Cassie, while I do a little exploring.

"You can't see a thing in this darkness!" Obediently Cassie groped for the top of the chest and sat. It creaked a little beneath her weight but held.

"There's a small crack of light at the top of the stairs," he pointed out absently.

"Only a cat could see anything in a place like this!"

"A cat or certain other creatures of the night, hmm?" His voice sounded more and more preoccupied and Cassie could hear him moving away from her.

"Justin, this is no time for Dracula jokes!"

"Sorry, honey. But it's not exactly a joke, is it? You see me as a kind of Dracula, don't you? Did you mean what you said earlier?"

"About not killing Reed? I certainly did! Furthermore—"

"Not that. About loving me."

"Oh, that." Where was he? Over by the stairs? How could he see anything in this endless night?

"Yes, that. Answer me, Cassie."

She took a deep breath. "I meant it, Justin."

"Then you and I have a lot to discuss when we get out of here, don't we?"

Cassie said nothing. Was that all she was going to get in exchange for a declaration of love? A "discussion?" But then, Justin didn't believe in love. From Justin she would get other things, like protection, loyalty, criticism of her creative efforts... "Oh, my God!" she suddenly yelped in a strangled voice, leaping to her feet.

"Cassie, what's wrong?" Justin's voice cut through the inky darkness like a whiplash.

"It's that damn cat," she said on a groan of relief as she identified the creature that had brushed against her leg. "Scared the you-know-what out of me. Thought it was a rat or something." She stooped over and located the cat's large body. He butted his head against her hand.

"How the hell did he get in here?" Justin was moving toward her. "That animal sure has a knack for getting around this house."

"Maybe he knows a few things we don't know. Like how to walk through walls."

''Maybe he does,'' Justin said thoughtfully. ''Too bad he can't talk.'' Sounding genuinely regretful, Justin moved off again, this time toward the far side of the staircase.

''What are you doing?'' Cassie asked softly, automatically continuing to pat the cat. It seemed to want attention and this was not the sort of cat you deliberately offended by disregarding such requests.

''Rigging a surprise for our friend Bailey. We have to get him to come into the basement and leave the door unlatched behind him. Won't do us any good to take care of him and have the door swing shut on us before we can get out. A man could pound on that door for a long time without making much of a dent in it.''

Cassie winced at the thought of being trapped in the basement. ''It's very reassuring to have you talk as if we could really take care of Bailey.'' The cat butted against her hand again and gave his rasping meow.

''We can take care of him if I just have enough time to sabotage this staircase.''

''I wonder why this stupid cat is suddenly getting so affectionate?''

''He's probably hungry and wants to know when you're going to feed him,'' Justin speculated idly. There was a sound of softly splintering wood.

''Justin, I— Damn it, cat! Can't you see that I'm in no position to feed you at the moment?''

The animal left her, meowing more loudly now. A moment later he returned, lashing his plump tail around her leg and then gliding off into the darkness again. Back and forth he went. Each time he returned to her it was with an increasing air of impatience.

Like a cat who wanted to be let of the house, Cassie thought suddenly. Back and forth from the door to the person who was supposed to open that door.

"Just how did you get into this basement?" Cassie whispered. She slid off the chest and crouched beside the animal. It was impossible to see the creature, but she could feel him sitting arrogantly at her feet.

With a rough little command the cat moved off again and this time Cassie kept a finger on his tail, hurrying after him. The creature stopped in front of what felt like a solid brick wall.

"Cassie? What are you doing?" Justin's voice came from the vicinity of the staircase.

"I don't know. This cat seems to want out and he's sitting in front of a bare wall as if he expects me to open it."

Justin came up beside her and she sensed him feeling the wall in front of the cat. "I wonder what he knows that we don't."

"Can you see anything?"

"No. There's not enough light this far from the staircase."

The cat gave a last demanding cry and disappeared.

"Justin!"

"I know." He crouched beside her. "Like you said, that cat knows how to walk through walls. What one creature of the night can do, two should be able to do."

Beside him Cassie, too, began feeling along the rough face of the basement wall. "It seems so solid!"

The words were hardly out of her mouth when her hand pushed against a surface that swung inward with astonishing ease. "Justin! Here!"

In an instant he was beside her. "A small door. It appears to be made out of wood. But I didn't see any break in the brick wall the last time I was down here with the flashlight... Come on, Cassie. The staircase trap might or might not have worked. This gives us a much more viable option."

"What? I don't understand." But he was already pushing her through the short door. She had to crouch to enter. On the other side her questing fingers found another staircase leading up out of the basement.

"Climb it very carefully. No telling what condition it's in. I'll be behind you if you lose your footing. And watch your head," Justin added with a muttered oath. A soft, painful-sounding thud suggested he had just learned about the low ceiling the hard way.

"Justin, there's a bit of light up ahead. It's from a door."

"Keep climbing. I'd like to get to the second level. It will give us an element of surprise. And keep your voice down."

Cassie obeyed because she could hear sounds now—the low murmur of voices. She tried to orient herself and finally decided that the door she was climbing past must open somewhere near the pantry, perhaps right into the pantry. With Justin close behind and making no sound at all, she obediently climbed up another level. Feeling with her hands along the wall, she found herself ascending a spiral staircase that was no more than a couple of feet wide.

The thinnest-possible crack of light revealed the next exit from the staircase. Cassie stopped in front of it.

"Here?" she breathed in the slightest of whispers.

"Here." Justin stepped carefully around her and pushed against the door. It swung inward easily. So easily that a cat might have managed the trick, too.

The black cat waited for them inside the room as Justin and Cassie emerged from the hidden panel.

"It's my closet!" Cassie mouthed, startled, as she glanced around. The hidden door was cut into the paneled walk-in closet, undetectable unless one knew exactly where to push.

Justin motioned her to silence, striding quickly into the room. All she could see was his dark shape as he moved toward the door. The cat was at his heels. They made a perfect pair.

"Justin?"

"Stay here, Cassie. We haven't got much time." Even as he spoke she heard the sound of a car pulling out of the drive. Reed Bailey's "business acquaintance," no doubt. With the other man gone, Bailey would be hurrying back to the basement to finish off the witnesses. He must know that even though Cassie and Justin didn't understand exactly what they had stumbled onto, they knew far too much. And they'd seen the gun in Bailey's hand.

Cassie hurried toward the door even as it closed behind Justin. She understood that Bailey had to be neutralized, but she also knew she must not let Justin kill him. There were limits to revenge.

Carefully she opened the door and slipped out into

the hall. Most of the house was still in darkness, although lights burned downstairs. She heard Bailey's heavy steps as he stalked below her toward the basement door. A moment later she heard the door being unlatched.

"All right, Drake. I've got a flashlight. You won't be able to hide in that basement. Believe me, I know every inch of it. Come on out and we'll get this over with quickly. If you don't, I'll just lock this door behind me and let you starve yourselves to death. Take your choice. I really don't much care... What the—"

Bailey's words ended in a muffled shout followed by the heavy thud of bodies crashing to the floor. The gun roared and Cassie flinched, conjuring up images of Justin lying dead on the parquet floor of the hall. She leaped to the railing and leaned over.

It wasn't Justin who lay on the wooden floor. It was Reed Bailey. And he couldn't shout again because Justin was straddling him, methodically cutting off his air supply with fiercely strong hands wrapped around his throat.

"Justin, no! Wait! Don't kill him!"

Cassie flew down the stairs, her heart pounding as she approached the violent scene. Justin didn't glance up. His face was set and implacable; more implacable than she had ever seen it.

"Justin, he's not worth it. Don't kill him! We'll get the police. It's gone far enough!"

"He tried to kill you," Justin said simply, tightening his hold on the other man's neck. It was obviously all the reason Justin needed to take Bailey's life. Even now Reed was turning a strange shade of purple. In another moment he would be unconscious and then dead.

"Justin, if you love me half as much as I love you, don't kill him!" Cassie begged. She stood horrified and desperate, knowing she didn't have the physical power to halt her lover if he chose to continue dealing out death.

Justin's head lifted then, and his dark eyes glittered with a feral fire. *"He tried to kill you."*

"You've saved me. Let that be the end of it. Justin, I love you. I don't want you to kill for me. There's no need. Not now. You've stopped him. You don't need revenge. Please, Justin. You don't need revenge. You have me, now."

For an instant longer the violent fire burned deep in his dark eyes and then Justin slowly looked down at his victim. Carefully, as if the process were incredibly difficult, he loosened his fingers from around Bailey's throat.

Reed gasped for air, his eyes bulging as he faced his would-be killer. The hallway reeked of Bailey's stark fear. He was well aware of his close call.

Justin got to his feet, the violence fading out of him slowly as he turned to face Cassie. His eyes continued to gleam with an intensity that was frightening, but the fires were no longer lethal.

"I love you," he whispered starkly.

Cassie smiled tremulously. "Yes. I know."

"I didn't realize... I thought it was all a myth." He shook his dark head once as if to clear it. "I knew I wanted you more than I'd ever wanted anything else on earth. But I didn't know it was love. Not until you used my love for you to stop me from doing something I thought I had to do.''

"I wasn't sure of just what you felt," she whispered. "But I know now."

He looked at her. "Yes." He frowned as Bailey made a move at his feet. "Come on. Let's get this fool to the sheriff's. There's another man to be caught and a lot of questions to be asked."

It was several hours later—Bailey was in jail and there was a bulletin out for the arrest of the man he had been more than willing to identify—when Justin drove Cassie back to the mansion on the cliff.

"Emeralds," Cassie said with an air of wonder. "Just think. If we'd spent a little more time exploring that basement we might have found them stashed in the chest Bailey used to hide them! It's all your fault, Justin. You're the one who wouldn't let me go back down the steps to the basement!"

He shot her a wry grin. "My fault, hmm?"

"Yes, but we'll let it pass," she decreed imperiously. "After all, how could you know that Bailey and his accomplice were gem smugglers?"

"The sheriff seemed just as surprised," Justin said. "Most stolen jewelry gets fenced through pawnbrokers or sold for only a fraction of its value on the streets. Bailey and his friend had a pretty ingenious system. The friend stole the stuff, gave it to Bailey to hide and then picked it up after the heat had died down. Then the stuff was taken to Canada and sold to a legitimate jeweler who thought he was buying legitimate, imported gems. Much higher profit margin.''

''Over the years they could have made a fortune. I'll bet Reed nearly had a fit when he got back from his last 'business' trip to discover his father had rented out the old house. Especially when he knew he had a visit from his accomplice due very shortly!''

''So he tried to frighten you out of the place by appearing on your balcony in the middle of the night and then leaving that old wedding gown.''

Cassie shuddered. Apparently Reed had not known of the secret stairway, but he'd confessed to climbing up the balcony to Cassie's room to terrorize her. The next time he'd seen her he'd made certain she heard the tale of Adeline and her lover. The step in the basement staircase had been weakened by Bailey a long time ago as a general precaution against anyone who might decide to explore the basement.

Justin guided the black Ferrari into the driveway and stopped the engine. The big black cat was sitting under the porte cochere waiting for them. He came forward as Cassie and Justin got out of the car and walked toward the entrance.

''I suppose he's upset because he never did get fed,'' Cassie observed as Justin opened the door and switched on the hall light. The cat traipsed in behind them.

''He deserves his reward.'' Justin leaned down to scratch the large animal behind the ears. ''You realize we'll have to take him with us when we leave?''

''I was rather hoping we could just close the door

on him and forget him,'' Cassie said dryly, eyeing the creature askance.

''Are you kidding? This is the kind of cat who would hunt you down and haunt you for the rest of your life if you tried a trick like that!''

''You'd know about that sort of revenge, would you?'' Cassie grinned, turning to wrap her arms around Justin's neck.

Justin's face went hard. ''I know about keeping the score even, Cassie. Yes, I know about revenge.'' His hands went to her waist, tightening almost painfully. ''Do you realize you're the only person in the whole world who could have stopped me from throttling Bailey?''

''I didn't want you killing anyone for me, Justin.''

''He deserved it. When he couldn't frighten you away from the house he invited us to that party so we'd be conveniently out when his accomplice was due to return for the gems. He should have let it go at that. He shouldn't have tried to get rid of you completely.''

Bailey hadn't cared particularly whether or not Cassie was killed in the fall from the cliff. He'd simply decided that such an event would cause sufficient chaos to ensure that he and his partner would not be bothered during the short time they needed to make the gem transaction. If the fall didn't kill her, he had figured it would cause enough injury to force her to return to San Francisco to recover. Justin, Bailey knew, would follow Cassie back to the city. It would get both of them out of the house permanently.

The gem transaction was only scheduled to last a

few minutes. Bailey had reasoned that he could slip away from the crowded party and return before anyone noticed the host was gone. Just in case someone did notice, he'd planned to return with a fresh pack of ice from the all-night machine near the market. Just the genial host slipping off to get some extra ice. No one would doubt him.

But Justin had headed straight back to the old mansion with Cassie as soon as he'd pulled her up from her rocky perch and that had spoiled all of Bailey's plans. He was very much the junior member of the smuggling partnership and more than a little nervous of his accomplice, who had a reputation for not tolerating mistakes. Bailey had had only a few minutes to figure out what to do with Justin and Cassie. So he'd shoved them in the basement and decided to kill them later.

"It's over now, Justin." Cassie stood on tiptoe to brush the gentlest of kisses across his hard mouth. "I think you're right, though. We do owe that cat something and he'll probably hold it over our heads for the rest of our lives."

"Speaking of the rest of our lives," Justin began quietly.

"Umm?"

"We will, of course, be spending them together."

"Will we?" she asked dreamily.

"Cassie, you're going to marry me." Justin's voice was dark and urgent.

"Justin, I can't give you what you want out of marriage. No one invites me to the right places or parties. I don't hang out with the upper-class, thoroughly respectable crowd you want to mingle with. My friends are very ordinary.'' She peered up at him anxiously, but he only smiled.

''I didn't know what I was looking for in life until I met you, Cassie. I thought I wanted status and respectability simply because it was something I didn't have. I didn't know what else to go looking for, I guess. Now I know that all I want is you.''

''You're sure, Justin?''

''I've never been more sure of anything,'' he vowed softly. ''What about you, Cassie? Do you know what you want?''

''I know I love you and that I trust you. I want very much to marry you.'' Her smile held the warmth of the sun.

''I think I'm going to like living in the sunlight,'' Justin whispered, folding her close and burying his lips in her tousled hair. ''Cassie, I swear you have nothing to fear from me. I'm as good at real estate investment as you are in the stock market. I don't need your money.''

''Real estate investment?'' she asked in surprise.

''Of course. You didn't really think I had no career, did you? And speaking of careers, I've been thinking about yours, and your talent for making money.''

''Which is boring.''

''Would it be boring if you used that talent to help other people make money?''

She lifted her head from his shoulder. ''What are you talking about?''

''Have you ever thought about making a career out of doing what you do best? Being a stock broker?

Think of how many people you could help by showing them how to make money in the market.''

Cassie tilted her head to one side, eyes wide in
surprise. "I never thought about that.''

"Between the two of us, we could offer a complete
financial-management package to people. How about
it, Cassie? Want to go into business with me?''

"The idea has a certain, inexplicable attraction.''
Cassie grinned. "Just like you yourself have.''

His hold on her tightened. "It's very late. Would
you care to come to bed and discuss the matter?''

"That depends. Are you going to sleep in the chair
again?''

Justin grinned: a slashing, thoroughly masculine
smile that held genuine laughter and a great deal of
love. "What do you think?'' He picked her up and
started toward the stairs.

"I think you have the world's most fantastic
teeth.'' Cassie laughed softly as the delicious longing
began to build in her body.

"And you have the most delightful throat. I think,
my sweet Cassie, that you and I were made for each
other.''

The ebony cat sat at the bottom of the stairs and
watched the two humans disappear into the east bedroom. Under normal circumstances he would have
made his demand for food a lot more vehement. The
relationship between himself and the two people at
the top of the stairs promised to be a long-term one,
however, and he could be indulgent at this stage.

In the east bedroom the first light of dawn was

beginning to touch the bed as Justin set Cassie down and began to undress her with reverent sensuality.

"I used to think of you as a creature of darkness," Cassie murmured as her clothing fell away beneath his touch.

"And I always thought of you as a creature of sunlight," Justin confided huskily. "Light and darkness go hand in hand, I've learned. One is meaningless without the other."

The two people who had found that for which they had been searching fused themselves together in a joyous bond that would last a lifetime.

* * * * *

You're not going to believe this offer!

In October and November 2000, buy any two Harlequin or Silhouette books and save $10.00 off future purchases, or buy any three and save $20.00 off future purchases!

Just fill out this form and attach 2 proofs of purchase (cash register receipts) from October and November 2000 books and Harlequin will send you a coupon booklet worth a total savings of $10.00 off future purchases of Harlequin and Silhouette books in 2001. Send us 3 proofs of purchase and we will send you a coupon booklet worth a total savings of $20.00 off future purchases.

Saving money has never been this easy.

I accept your offer! Please send me a coupon booklet:

Name: _____

Address: _____ City: _____

State/Prov.: _____ Zip/Postal Code: _____

Optional Survey!

In a typical month, how many Harlequin or Silhouette books would you buy <u>new</u> at retail stores?

☐ Less than 1   ☐ 1   ☐ 2   ☐ 3 to 4   ☐ 5+

Which of the following statements best describes how you <u>buy</u> Harlequin or Silhouette books? Choose one answer only that <u>best</u> describes you.

☐ I am a regular buyer and reader
☐ I am a regular reader but buy only occasionally
☐ I only buy and read for specific times of the year, e.g. vacations
☐ I subscribe through Reader Service but also buy at retail stores
☐ I mainly borrow and buy only occasionally
☐ I am an occasional buyer and reader

Which of the following statements best describes how you <u>choose</u> the Harlequin and Silhouette series books you buy <u>new</u> at retail stores? By "series," we mean books within a particular line, such as *Harlequin PRESENTS* or *Silhouette SPECIAL EDITION*. Choose one answer only that <u>best</u> describes you.

☐ I only buy books from my favorite series
☐ I generally buy books from my favorite series but also buy
    books from other series on occasion
☐ I buy some books from my favorite series but also buy from
    many other series regularly
☐ I buy all types of books depending on my mood and what
    I find interesting and have no favorite series

Please send this form, along with your cash register receipts as proofs of purchase, to:
In the U.S.: Harlequin Books, P.O. Box 9057, Buffalo, NY 14269
In Canada: Harlequin Books, P.O. Box 622, Fort Erie, Ontario L2A 5X3
(Allow 4-6 weeks for delivery) Offer expires December 31, 2000.

PHQ4002